Anthony Gilbert and The Murder Room

>>> This title is part of The Murder Room, our series dedicated to making available out-of-print or hard-to-find titles by classic crime writers.

Crime fiction has always held up a mirror to society. The Victorians were fascinated by sensational murder and the emerging science of detection; now we are obsessed with the forensic detail of violent death. And no other genre has so captivated and enthralled readers.

Vast troves of classic crime writing have for a long time been unavailable to all but the most dedicated frequenters of second-hand bookshops. The advent of digital publishing means that we are now able to bring you the backlists of a huge range of titles by classic and contemporary crime writers, some of which have been out of print for decades.

From the genteel amateur private eyes of the Golden Age and the femmes fatales of pulp fiction, to the morally ambiguous hard-boiled detectives of mid twentieth-century America and their descendants who walk our twenty-first century streets, The Murder Room has it all. **>>>**

The Murder Room
Where Criminal Minds Meet

themurderroom.com

Anthony Gilbert (1899–1973)

Anthony Gilbert was the pen name of Lucy Beatrice Malleson. Born in London, she spent all her life there, and her affection for the city is clear from the strong sense of character and place in evidence in her work. She published 69 crime novels, 51 of which featured her best known character, Arthur Crook, a vulgar London lawyer totally (and deliberately) unlike the aristocratic detectives, such as Lord Peter Wimsey, who dominated the mystery field at the time. She also wrote more than 25 radio plays, which were broadcast in Great Britain and overseas. Her thriller *The Woman in Red* (1941) was broadcast in the United States by CBS and made into a film in 1945 under the title *My Name is Julia Ross*. She was an early member of the British Detection Club, which, along with Dorothy L. Sayers, she prevented from disintegrating during World War II. Malleson published her autobiography, *Three-a-Penny*, in 1940, and wrote numerous short stories, which were published in several anthologies and in such periodicals as *Ellery Queen's Mystery Magazine* and *The Saint*. The short story 'You Can't Hang Twice' received a Queens award in 1946. She never married, and evidence of her feminism is elegantly expressed in much of her work.

By Anthony Gilbert

Scott Egerton series

Tragedy at Freyne (1927)

The Murder of Mrs
   Davenport (1928)

Death at Four Corners (1929)

The Mystery of the Open
   Window (1929)

The Night of the Fog (1930)

The Body on the Beam (1932)

The Long Shadow (1932)

The Musical Comedy
   Crime (1933)

An Old Lady Dies (1934)

The Man Who Was Too
   Clever (1935)

Mr Crook Murder
   Mystery series

Murder by Experts (1936)

The Man Who Wasn't
   There (1937)

Murder Has No Tongue (1937)

Treason in My Breast (1938)

The Bell of Death (1939)

Dear Dead Woman (1940)
   aka *Death Takes a Redhead*

The Vanishing Corpse (1941)
   aka *She Vanished in the Dawn*

The Woman in Red (1941)
   aka *The Mystery of the
   Woman in Red*

Death in the Blackout (1942)
   aka *The Case of the Tea-
   Cosy's Aunt*

Something Nasty in the
   Woodshed (1942)
   aka *Mystery in the Woodshed*

The Mouse Who Wouldn't
   Play Ball (1943)
   aka *30 Days to Live*

He Came by Night (1944)
   aka *Death at the Door*

The Scarlet Button (1944)
   aka *Murder Is Cheap*

A Spy for Mr Crook (1944)

The Black Stage (1945)
   aka *Murder Cheats the Bride*

Don't Open the Door (1945)
   aka *Death Lifts the Latch*

Lift Up the Lid (1945)
   aka *The Innocent Bottle*

The Spinster's Secret (1946)
   aka *By Hook or by Crook*

Death in the Wrong Room
   (1947)

Die in the Dark (1947)
   aka *The Missing Widow*

Death Knocks Three Times
   (1949)

Murder Comes Home (1950)

A Nice Cup of Tea (1950)
   aka *The Wrong Body*

Lady-Killer (1951)

Miss Pinnegar Disappears (1952)
 aka *A Case for Mr Crook*

Footsteps Behind Me (1953)
 aka *Black Death*

Snake in the Grass (1954)
 aka *Death Won't Wait*

Is She Dead Too? (1955)
 aka *A Question of Murder*

And Death Came Too (1956)

Riddle of a Lady (1956)

Give Death a Name (1957)

Death Against the Clock (1958)

Death Takes a Wife (1959)
 aka *Death Casts a Long Shadow*

Third Crime Lucky (1959)
 aka *Prelude to Murder*

Out for the Kill (1960)

She Shall Die (1961)
 aka *After the Verdict*

Uncertain Death (1961)

No Dust in the Attic (1962)

Ring for a Noose (1963)

The Fingerprint (1964)

The Voice (1964)
 aka *Knock, Knock! Who's There?*

Passenger to Nowhere (1965)

The Looking Glass Murder (1966)

The Visitor (1967)

Night Encounter (1968)
 aka *Murder Anonymous*

Missing from Her Home (1969)

Death Wears a Mask (1970)
 aka *Mr Crook Lifts the Mask*

Murder is a Waiting Game (1972)

Tenant for the Tomb (1971)

A Nice Little Killing (1974)

Standalone Novels

The Case Against Andrew Fane (1931)

Death in Fancy Dress (1933)

The Man in the Button Boots (1934)

Courtier to Death (1936)
 aka *The Dover Train Mystery*

The Clock in the Hatbox (1939)

Riddle of a Lady

Anthony Gilbert

An Orion book

Copyright © Lucy Beatrice Malleson 1956

The right of Lucy Beatrice Malleson to be identified as the author of this work has been asserted in accordance with the Copyright, Designs and Patents Act 1988.

This edition published by
The Orion Publishing Group Ltd
Orion House
5 Upper St Martin's Lane
London WC2H 9EA

An Hachette UK company
A CIP catalogue record for this book is available from the British Library

ISBN 978 1 4719 1006 7

www.orionbooks.co.uk

CHAPTER I

THE FIRM of Greatorex Brothers attained legal eminence in London almost a century ago, but the Beckfield branch was opened in 1930, ostensibly because London could no longer handle the great volume of business that came its way, but actually to provide a niche for young Henry Greatorex, who had proved himself an intolerable thorn in the side of his sober half-brothers, Richard and Charles.

" Henry doesn't seem to realise the law is a serious profession," they confided to each other. " Clients expect a responsible bearing, they need to feel their own importance. They put themselves and their affairs in our hands—Henry is altogether too casual . "

" Too easy in his manner . . ."

" Too lounging . . . too quizzical . . . insolent, really, in a fellow his age . . ."

In short, Henry was light upon the weights. Obviously he must be provided for; all the Greatorexes had a great sense of family, and he couldn't altogether be blamed for his frivolous attitude towards life. That, said the tight-lipped brothers, who looked part of their background, like the ponderous crystal chandeliers, the handsome carpets, the period tables and chairs, was, in part at least, the fault of his parent, that extraordinary woman their father had married at a time when he might have been looking for grandsons. The brothers had always known no good would come of that. What had come were Christopher, destined to lie, thirty years later, in a nameless Spanish grave, dead fighting for a cause not even his own, and Henry, who seemed to think that poise and charm and the most indifferent knowledge of law were enough to establish your relations with your clients.

Not the least of the brothers' grievances was the fact that, in Henry's case, they had been.

Twenty years of running the Beckfield office had put

1

a touch of grey in Henry's hair, but had neither stooped his shoulders nor lined his cool, humorous face. On the twentieth anniversary of his coming to Beckfield his staff gave him a luncheon at the Bull, that ancient inn where highwaymen were once sheltered by an enterprising landlady who wasn't above planting them in her bed and identifying each as her husband. Beckfield, for all its importance as a thriving market town, had the same air of composure as Henry had. Young Avery Greatorex, Christopher's only son, who had reached Beckfield some three months earlier, via the D.P. camps of Europe, where he'd unaccountably lingered after the end of the war, sat at the foot of the table and heard one member of the staff after another rise and offer a tribute to the guest of honour. He rubbed his eyes, feeling that nothing about him was quite real. Beckfield appeared to him as a little pocket of unbelievable peace; the war seemed to have passed it by. He looked through the latticed windows to the green beyond, where four geese processed solemnly down to the pond; and he heard, with a sort of scornful wonder, old Mr. Hall announcing that, like Drake, he would rise from his grave if ever Greatorex Brothers, by which, of course, he meant Henry, needed him. Mr. Hall had been employed by the firm for thirty-seven years, and, if strength were granted him, he said, he'd be happy to serve them for another thirty-seven. He was a little waxy man, with a spruce white moustache, and his gaze, resting on Henry, wasn't far short of hero worship.

How Henry could take it without squirming was more than Avery could understand. For these compliments, so innocently and devotedly offered to him, weren't spoken with the tongue in the cheek. " He's bamboozled them all till they really believe what they say," Avery reflected, leaning back in his chair, tall and fair and more like his distinguished-looking uncle than he'd ever know. For Avery knew, if no one else did, that the columns of the firm weren't himself and Uncle Henry, but old Mr. Hall and Miss Bainbridge, Uncle Henry's devoted middle-aged secretary, in her brown dress, with her neat speckled hair and her hands trembling, because in a minute she was going to rise and return thanks for the female staff. Mr. Hall might stay late four nights out of five, Miss Bainbridge took work home at week-ends, but as the clock struck five, rain or shine Henry capped his pen, took his hat from the hook, his stick from the stand and, suave, benevolent, smiling—Peter Pan grown up, thought the disapproving Avery—he would make his way through the central office, followed by the smiles and good wishes of everyone present.

" Feudal," reflected Avery. " Why do they stand for it? "

The idea that charm of itself was enough to win you a bread ticket should have been exploded long ago, but here was the old man exploiting his undoubted gifts and getting away with it a hundred times out of a hundred.

Old Uncle Humbug, Old Uncle Handsome, he thought, old King Charmer at his best, smiling encouragingly at Miss Bainbridge as she rose and clutched the back of her chair to reinforce her courage. Miss Bainbridge was nervous. Henry was her life. Avery knew that if nobody else did. Where most people look forward to the week-end, Miss Bainbridge counted the hours to Monday morning. If Henry was away with a cold or on business the sun went out of her sky; she just ploughed through the day and counted the hours till morning. She was a few years Henry's senior and used to cry scornfully that she couldn't understand this ridiculous demand for pensions for spinsters at fifty-five; why, fifty-five was no age at all. Now she pushed her glasses into place and looked about her rather wildly. Her brows were creased with anxiety; this was her great moment. Still, wondered Avery, must she look so like a messenger of doom? Henry smiled again. Wicked old Henry, the bachelor but surely not the celibate. Avery could believe a good deal, knowing at least there are plenty of things too bad to be true, but he couldn't swallow that. Women must have been trailing after Henry since he got into long trousers, but

3

he wasn't married and it didn't seem likely he'd get caught now. Too lazy, probably, couldn't cope with school bills and sickness and a woman's moods and being tied by the heels, having to go to the seaside and play cricket on the sands instead of stepping into a B.O.A.C. airliner and floating off into the void without a care on earth. Mr. Hall and Miss Bainbridge might wonder how the work was getting on without them, but Avery was prepared to swear Henry didn't even remember the existence of the office when he was away from it.

Suddenly he stiffened. Something had caught his attention, as a motorist, making a good pace, is suddenly aware he's passed a landmark without being quite sure what it is. He hadn't been listening very carefully to what the old dear was saying; he thought he could have written her speech himself. But she had just said something of real import and the maddening thing was he couldn't be sure what it was. Only, like an unexpected nettle stinging you into awareness, he knew something had happened he oughtn't to overlook. He set himself to recall the words. The impression he had was one of danger. Miss Bainbridge had been speaking to the room at large during the earlier part of her speech, but those last words had been directed clear at Henry. Avery glanced up the length of the table, but there was no change in Henry's expression. He was regarding Miss Bainbridge with a kind of tenderness, nothing so arrogant as compassion, a friendliness that, real or assumed, was the root of his success. It was a manner he could switch on as easily as you put on an electric light. Only with a light you get warmth and was there anything behind Henry's apparent interest? The fact is, Avery decided, we none of us know anything about him, and it occurred to him, for the first time, that perhaps he, Avery, was the noodle, the nincompoop, and that easy-going casual charming Henry was the most subtle Greatorex of them all.

Meantime, there was that warning that Henry was steering for danger—it never occurred to him that Miss

Bainbridge might be mistaken. She knew something, though he hadn't a notion what it was. Only what she was trying to say was that life's a two-sided medal and you can't win all the time—in short, that the Old Man had an enemy and he'd better watch out. Incorrigibly, Avery felt his interest quicken, for who was going to dislike Henry or wish him harm? Or (and here Avery chuckled to himself) perhaps old Uncle Charming had been cooking the books all these years (Avery wouldn't put it past him and what a joke he'd think it) and Miss Bainbridge was warning him that someone was on his trail.

And now, at last, it was Henry's turn. He came leisurely to his feet, the romantic, the unknown, the go-getter, about whom almost anything could be true.

First of all he thanked them for their hospitality. " I'm only sorry," said he, " that my brothers couldn't be here for the occasion. It must be as much of a surprise to them as it is to me to realise how safely I am dug in here after twenty years. I don't mind confessing to you now that when they put me into Beckfield, when I was about the same age as my nephew here (and his glance added, impishly, that Avery had probably been despatched to this branch office for precisely the same reason, that he got in the old men's hair) they were drawing lots as to which of them should come down and pull the chestnuts out of the fire within twelve months. As a matter of fact, they weren't required, because we had such excellent chestnut-pullers on the spot. Mr. Hall, Miss Bainbridge, there's no need for me to tell the rest of you that the firm's reputation is in their hands rather than mine. They've given me a lot to-day, but the younger generation (and here he grinned openly at Avery) know where that credit really belongs. When I came here my brother Charles gave me a piece of advice that, he said, was worth a fortune. Nothing, he assured me, can be achieved without hard work." Someone started to clap and Henry waited politely till the applause had died down. " That's perfectly true, but what he didn't add was that it needn't of necessity be your own work. Omar Khayyám says something about taking the cash and letting the credit go. Bad economics, ladies and gentlemen. A sound economist sees to it that he gets cash and credit, both. And I think I may claim some success in the sphere of economics. For twenty years I've had the best of both worlds. I've sat in the handsomest room in the office and let other people work to support me. Does that seem immoral to you? But you've just heard our two principal speakers proclaim that they enjoy work and I enjoy the fruits of that work, so we are all satisfied. Personally I shall be content to continue in our respective roles for another twenty years, if I am spared, and I shall be ungrateful indeed if I make a premature departure from the scene, realising how many people are anxious to preserve my existence from overwork. And I can only hope that twenty years from now you will all be as satisfied with your dividends as, I am convinced, I shall be with mine."

He sat down to laughter and applause. Avery was aware of a sudden anger. He realised he'd under-estimated Uncle Henry. It was a case of deliberate exploitation; he couldn't guess how romantic and hand-some and like his uncle he seemed, leaning back with one arm thrown over the back of his chair and a flush of indignation in his thin cheeks. All about him murmurs arose of congratulation and self-depreciation, and people were crowding Henry and there was any amount of hand-shaking and Miss Bainbridge actually had tears in her fine brown eyes behind the thick glasses. Then, thank goodness, before they could fall, the coffee came round, brought in by the landlord himself, and with it a bottle of rare old liqueur, wasted on most of those present, Avery reflected, feeling as starchy as his own forebear, who had died in the Smithfield fires sooner than recant a jot of his stiff-necked faith. The party broke up, people formed into little groups. Henry, coffee cup in hand, walked round, talking to everyone in turn. For a lazy man he seemed to know a remarkable amount about the individual's affairs. Avery was surprised again. He couldn't accept the fact that Henry had that qualification that no intellect, no hard work or integrity can replace—an ability to put himself in another man's shoes.

" Henry will never get the best out of a staff," Richard Greatorex had said disapprovingly to his brother, Charles. " He doesn't put the firm first."

He was right, of course. Henry believed in the rights of the individual. When he interviewed clients he gave the impression that this was the one case of hardship or injustice to engage his attention. It was the equivalent of what, in doctors, is known as a bedside manner. Henry had it to perfection. What lay beneath it Avery hadn't, at this date, the slightest idea.

On the way back to the office he contrived to walk with Miss Bainbridge.

" Tell me something," he said. " What were you warning Uncle Henry against? "

He saw apprehension leap into the brown eyes; her voice came quick and low.

" Mr. Avery, you're one of the family. Perhaps you could drop him a hint—that things aren't always what they seem, I mean—and it doesn't do to trust everybody. He wouldn't think—being so sympathetic and un-selfseeking (this was almost enough to make Avery puke) —that everyone isn't the same. And jealousy's a dreadful thing. It's like a knife in your back, it could even *be* a knife in your back . . ."

" You know, if I had the smallest idea what you were talking about we could get on faster," suggested Avery, pleasantly. " Who's jealous? "

She hesitated, coloured unbecomingly, then muttered something about a woman. Ho, ho, thought Avery, so he's not impervious after all. This'll make the uncles in London sit up. But how on earth . . . ? How on earth did Miss Bainbridge know anything about it, he meant? Whether she really knew anything or whether she was building some fancy situation with no foundation in fact he couldn't yet determine, and before he could put

7

another question to her, Henry came strolling up and joined them.

"I hope my nephew isn't trying to demoralise you, Miss Bainbridge," he remarked. "He doesn't approve of me, you know. Not his fault, of course. He's just a product of his generation. He doesn't remember a world where leisure was as necessary as air. We've reached a stage in our social development where conscientious people have an actual sense of guilt if they're not working practically all their waking hours."

"You've got us wrong, Uncle Henry," said Avery coolly. "Miss Bainbridge and I enjoy ourselves in our own way, which is by working. We shouldn't get any fun out of grasshoppering . . ."

"Two industrious emmets," Henry grinned. "You should try grasshoppering some time, though. There's something very pleasant about the hot sun and the nice whirring noise in the grass. After all, if you've never tried the joys of idleness you're in much the same position as a man who's never tasted anything but roast beef and swears it's the best dish in the world. It would be just as fair to say it was the worst. Rejoice, oh young man, in thy youth, and don't be a slave to duty, Miss Bainbridge. You're a positive reproach to me, I swear you are."

"Oh, Mr. Henry." (She always called him that, having worked in the London office for the first two years of her service with the Greatorexes.) "I could never be happy doing nothing."

"An acquired taste," Henry agreed. "But I can see I'm wasting my time."

Someone else came up and he moved away. "Do you know the only thing that really frightens me?" Miss Bainbridge inquired of Avery. "The thought that one day I may have to give up work, because I shall be past it. I do try to think up hobbies, but it's no use. My last prayer every night is that I shall die in harness."

It seemed to Avery quite probable that this was one of

those prayers that would be answered, certainly if Uncle H. had anything to do with it.

Up in London the brothers were solemnly toasting Henry in a glass of excellent port.

" I take off my hat to him, as they say nowadays," acknowledged Charles. " I never thought he'd stick it."

" Oh, Henry's full of surprises," Richard growled. " We haven't had the last, you mark my words."

" What have you in mind now? " his brother wanted to know.

They looked like a pair off 'Forsyte 'Change, both impeccably dressed and turned out, leisured, dignified, never touching dubious business, their reputation as spotless as the linen they changed every morning. They were both widowers—(Greatorex wives have a way of predeceasing their husbands, one day the police ought to look into it, commented Henry irreverently), Charles, childless all his days, Richard with a boy who had fallen at Dunkirk and an only daughter married and on the other side of the world. Avery was their hope now, and he was a dark horse, too. Charles said as much.

" The last of the Greatorexes," he observed.

Richard sprang his mine. " I wouldn't be too sure. Henry always had the capacity to consume his own smoke. Did it occur to you that this decision of Graham Carr to take his daughter on a cruise was a bit sudden? "

Charles looked astounded. " You mean Henry—and Beverley Carr? But she's young enough to be his daughter."

" Oh, Henry's ageless. That's part of his charm. The year he was with us he could do anything he liked with the staff. They never made any secret of it, and it went for the men as well as the women. And I don't doubt it's been precisely the same at Beckfield. Walking through the street with Henry is like attending a civic reception. I suggested to him it might be simpler for him to carry his hat, save him the trouble of taking it off every thirty seconds, but he said if he had it in his hand he couldn't raise it, and they're old-fashioned at Beckfield. To be candid with you, Chas, I've often wondered how he contrived to stay single so long."

"And now this girl!" Charles still could scarcely accept it.

"Mind you, I can't answer for Henry. But Graham told me in confidence *she's* completely infatuated. He wants to give her a chance to see things straight, and really one can scarcely blame him. I wouldn't have wanted Moira to marry a man five-and-twenty years older than herself. In point of fact, he was trying to pump me."

"To know if Henry had dropped a hint ?"

"Precisely. I had to tell him I knew nothing, but that if Henry wanted to marry Beverley he'd go straight to the fountain-head."

"And does he?" Charles reflected.

"Your guess is as good as mine. But he made one rather cryptic remark last time I saw him. A man only starts to get old when he becomes incapable of change, he said. I admit that might mean nothing coming from an ordinary man, but, for all his casual airs, Henry doesn't often say a thing for the pleasure of hearing his own voice. As they say on the stage, he throws whole sentences away. But that doesn't imply they're valueless."

"And Graham? Did he give any idea of his attitude?"

"The girl's all he has, he wants her happiness above all things. And if Henry is her happiness, he'd not stand in their way. And if our younger brother sets himself to get a thing, I've never known him to fail. I tell you, the whole of Beckfield would go into mourning if anything happened to Henry. Chris was the same. They get it from that mother of theirs, I suppose." He thought of his own mother and Charles's, an upright uncompromising woman who wouldn't have crossed the road to speak to her husband's second choice.

"If you're right, this is going to put young Avery's nose out of joint," Charles murmured, but Richard replied that he had no particular confidence in Avery.

He was like Henry in that he didn't consider law the last word—just a pack of rules put together by fallible men for their self-protection, he'd call it. "No," he assured his brother, "Henry's son may inherit the business yet, and, if he does, Avery will walk out without a care in the world. He's like his father there. No proper sense of values. As for Henry, if he wants this girl, he'll have her. On my Sam, I believe that chap could get away with murder."

Back in the office Henry uncapped his pen, put some correspondence conveniently to hand, took a sheet of plain paper from a stationery rack and settled down to think about Beverley. He was under no illusions whatsoever as to Graham Carr's motive in swooping down and whisking his daughter off to the Canaries. And, as it happened, this suited Henry's book very well. Not that he was in any doubt about his own feelings. There was a song you sometimes heard on the wireless about the breeze whispering Louise, only in his case it whispered—no, shouted—Beverley. From their first meeting, three months earlier, he had known here was his fate. He'd managed to side-step quite a number of excellent chances during the past twenty years, had thought it likely he'd go unwed to the grave, but his first sight of Beverley changed all that. He knew there was more than twenty years between them but he didn't propose to let that stand in his way. The obvious Greatorex to suit her, if she was going to marry into the family, was Avery, but, thought Henry, quite dispassionate, quite cool, if she so much as looks in his direction I shall take my nephew out to lunch and without any hesitation dunk a dose of poison in his coffee, or invite him to come walking with me and push him off a cliff, or . . . He laughed then. Avery wasn't going to have the chance of marrying Beverley, because if Henry didn't marry her no one should. He didn't know what she felt, couldn't speak to her father for her till he'd cleared up some loose ends that might trip them both if they weren't tidied out of the way. And he proposed to start the tidying process to-night. In a word, he had to clear up the business of Stella.

At approximately the same time, three other people had Henry in the front of their minds, three people whose future was to be closely knit with his.

In the Customs shed Beverley Carr watched the officials sign her baggage for removal to the ship. Three months ago she'd have been mad with excitement at the thought of this cruise—the only child of a widower absorbed in his own concerns, her life had been a very quiet one— but now everything was different. Now her troubled heart beat like a piston-rod. *Hen-ry. Hen-ry. Hen-ry.* Surely he couldn't be indifferent and yet—he'd said nothing, had seemed almost pleased, when he learned of her plans. Whenever she heard his name her own heart plunged and then seemed to stop beating, because this time, this time, she might hear he was going to marry someone whose name wasn't Beverley Carr.

" If I don't marry him I shall die an old maid," she told her reflection in the glass. She'd never understood love could do this to you, had thought it fun to have young men laying their hearts at her feet; she had tried to be kind and not lead them on. And now she was the rejected one. She was certain he didn't care. Love had made her humble; she didn't guess how humble it made Henry, too.

Her father's hand closed on her arm. " Toothache, Beverley? "

" Of course not." Don't let Father guess. Father must never guess. She looked round in a sprightly fashion. No doubt there'd be a score of charmers on board who'd manage to drive Henry's image out of her heart. She inspected them all that first night at dinner and, having done so, sympathised with the man who, married to a plain woman, stood his wife in the hall-stand and took his umbrella to bed.

In their little house at Burns Row, Martindale, William

Lockyer said to his wife, "What's the time, Martha?"

"It's not four yet. You get a bit of sleep before Mr. Browne comes or you won't beat him at chess to-night."

"If he comes."

"Now, Will, why do we have to have this every week? He's been coming for five years, except when he's been on holiday or sick, and then he's always let us know."

"Can't think why he troubles," said Will Lockyer, who had had one of his bad nights and was now scarcely ever free from pain. "He's a good chap, Martha."

"He comes to get a handsome game of chess," insisted Martha, loyally. "He says so himself. People don't play chess any more, it's all this canasta and television."

"It was good of him to bring us the TV set. It's what I've always said. You get the real old type of officer . . ."

Martha nodded. She'd heard it all before, but she was patient, because she knew she couldn't have stood it if she'd been in Will's place. Thirty-five years of ill-health, ten more years than he'd had of being like other men. That first war had a lot to answer for. And the last ten years hardly out of bed one day in four and now not above a dozen hours a week; and the doctor said he was bound to go downhill from now on. And people were busy, not unkind, but kept themselves to themselves, and everybody has their troubles, and a bedridden man can't join in general conversation, I mean, you have to be so careful, not say the wrong thing. There are so many words you mustn't use. Cripple was one; and jokes about impotence, meaning no harm, of course, the way most men didn't, but when you were like poor Will you seemed to have lost more than the use of your limbs. You lost a skin, things that slipped off another man were like knives to you. She was as grateful to Henry Browne as Will was. Friday nights were the highlight of the week. He always stayed an hour, sometimes more, which gave her a chance to slip down to the Ladies' Bar at the Coach and Horses, with Mrs. Hope and Mrs. Worsley, just for a change. She had never been a drinking woman—a half pint of stout saw her through the evening—but, oh, the break and the refreshment of that blessed hour every Friday night. And the magazines he brought, the kind with shiny pages, not old ones he'd done with, but brand-new, not even read. And the way he and Will nattered away on subjects you couldn't expect a woman to understand, the state of the world and research and all those bodies and societies you only knew by initials and they didn't convey anything to you, not really—Mr. Browne had them all at the tip of his tongue.

"Now you get a bit of shut-eye," she coaxed her husband, "and I'll start getting the supper ready. You know he's always here at six, and you'll see, he'll be here to-night same as every other Friday."

That evening, in a house not a mile away from the Lockyers', Stella Foster put on her new green dress and contemplated the evening's possibilities. Stella was that displaced person in modern social life, the deserted married woman who has never sued for divorce and is no longer in a position to do so. When Henry first met her, five years earlier, she had reminded him of one of the figures in Botticelli's "Primavera." She had yellow hair without a hint of gold in it, and eyes of a strange lucent green set a little aslant under smooth fair brows. Her face was rather long, with beautifully-moulded temples and cheekbones, she had a Mona Lisa mouth and a great air of repose. And yet, under the quiet and the promise of peace, life stirred vigorously, just as it burns and labours under the tranquil earth when the sap goes racing through the bough and the flower unfurls from the sheath. Mind you, his feeling for her had never been what he now felt for Beverley. Here, he had thought, was the adventure to be taken in hand and enjoyed, never the promise of a new life that could only be swallowed up by the grave. Since he met Beverley he had begun to think the old die-hards like his brothers had something, after all, with their rigid belief in the immortality of the soul and eternal life. Hitherto, he couldn't imagine any power of creation who would want to preserve casual, lazy Henry Greatorex after the breath had left his body, but Henry and Beverley together would become an expression of that love that is imperishable. For the first time in his life he discovered the truth of the saying that it is not good for man to live alone. Man alone was nothing until he was transfigured by love, love for a woman, an ideal, a God. For him immortality had taken the shape of Beverley Carr. None of this knowledge had been vouchsafed him when he encountered Stella. It was the merest chance they had met at all, and she gave him the most delightful sensation, like being in a cool wood, where no fierce winds penetrated the branches and even the bird-song was subdued. He met her again and again, learned a little about her.

" I'm married," she told him frankly. " It didn't last. Sydney wasn't the marrying sort. He did warn me but I wouldn't listen. I was over the moon with love. He blew off after about a year, and I've hardly heard from him since. No, we never tried for a divorce, either of us, because it came to me I'm not really the marrying kind either."

She had a small dressmaking business, was what's known as a " little woman ", and a little money she had inherited. She worked during the day and went out with friends in the evening. No, she was not too lonely. It was not a bad life. When he got to know her better he understood about that. She attracted people, men in particular, as the sun attracts the bud. She couldn't go into a saloon bar—at the Coach and Horses, say, or the Horn of Plenty—without someone coming along and wanting to buy her a drink. They were her version of the Women's Institute, she said. Henry reserved his comments, only assuring himself she didn't know much about women's institutes. And she made her own clothes and liked cooking—taking one thing with another, she made out. Within a few weeks they had become lovers.

Henry set her up in a little house in Hallett Street and she kept on with her dressmaking more for the company it implied than anything else, and he visited her pretty often at first, but cooled off fairly soon. Still, she

15

was good company and charming to look at, and experienced in all the ways that bind men. She kept him away from other women, too, and one way and another the affair ran on very accommodatingly for five years or so. Henry wasn't jealous and if he suspected she was not altogether faithful to him he kept that to himself. Stella was no fool either; she had known for twelve months at least that it was only his lazy good nature and his excellent manners that kept him coming so steadily every Friday, regular as clockwork. In the contrary order of things, as his indifference grew her passion quickened. She knew exactly when he met Beverley, there was a change in him, a warmth, an urgency that had never been for her. Not that he ever dropped a hint. Come to that, he had always been remarkably secretive about his private life, and even now she did not realise that his main desire was to preserve that privacy; he did not want even attractive women like Stella, well-meaning devoted women like Addie Bainbridge, straying through the passages of his mind, peeping through his secret doors. He remained urbane, courteous, charming, but always a mystery, even after five years.

CHAPTER II

HENRY GREATOREX had a service flat in a compact building on the farther side of Beckfield. It was about a quarter of a mile from his office, and he would come swinging out in the morning, as ready for the new day as a schoolboy on Saturday morning. He didn't run a car, saying he owed it to his figure to keep on his own feet. That might have seemed odd in anyone else, but Henry was a law to himself. On this momentous night, that was to transform his world, he reached home soon after five, poured himself out his customary glass of sherry, but a little earlier than usual, and changed his grey suit for a beautifully-cut country tweed. He pitched his silver-grey hat on to a shelf, and put on a soft chocolate-coloured monstrosity (the London brothers would have said) and, every inch the country squire, prepared for the evening. He shaved for the second time that day, being what Arthur Crook, that least conventional of lawyers, would have called a fussy fellow, a descendant of dandies and still aware of his ancestry. Dusting the talcum powder over his chin he found himself wishing for once that the evening was well over. He was a lazy chap and hated trouble. If he weren't, he could have eased himself out of this situation a couple of years ago, but he liked things to be pleasant, and why hurt anyone's feelings if it can be helped? So he had drifted until now he found himself on the edge of the rapids, and by no means certain that he was going to come through un-scathed. Ah, well, trust to his luck, which had stood him pretty well up to the present; and maybe Stella would meet him half-way.

As Crook would have observed—And how!

A pile of new glossy magazines and periodicals lay on a table in the hall, and he scooped them up on his way out. He walked across the little common past the Duck and Six Drakes where the bus pulled up, arriving thirty seconds before it appeared round the bend. There were several people waiting, but he found a seat and was surprised and not too pleased to hear someone say his name. It was his nephew, Avery, accompanied by a handsome solid-looking Scotch terrier, with the moustaches of a guardee and eyebrows a prawn might envy. He sat very square and erect in the passageway of the bus, magnificently unaware of everyone.

" Yours? " asked Henry, rather astonished.

" By adoption and grace. I should introduce you. Meet Mr. Smith. He belonged to the previous tenants at my lodgings, but they couldn't be bothered with him. Gave him a seat in the window, two meals a day and a run to the pillar box morning and night, and thought they'd done their duty by him. When they went away they left Mr. Smith behind with a roll of old carpet and a lot of newspapers."

" So you took him on? You're your father's son all right. Ever think of being a parson? " he added, keenly.

Avery felt the colour mount to his cheeks. Typical of the Old Man to hit the nail on the head without even trying.

" Yes," he admitted, hoping he betrayed none of his inward confusion. " Too much red tape," he added. " Exams and so forth."

Henry nodded. " I know." What did he know? That it hadn't been the exams that had frightened Avery? It was uncanny how he could probe to the heart of your mystery with scarcely a word said. Still, that decision was one he didn't propose to discuss in any quarter. Stooping, he gently touched the dog's head.

" He was a bit upstage to start with, and no wonder. He'd been led up the garden before. I gather they were all over him the first year. He's rising four now."

" He looks like the eye that never sleeps," Henry admitted. " You must have a remarkably clear conscience, Avery. Look out, you'll have to pull him in. This chap wants to collect the fares."

Avery, however, made no move. The dog wasn't on a lead. As the conductor approached, he moved his handsome head, shifted a great ebony paw.

"Thanks, old chap," said the conductor. It was clear Mr. Smith had already clarified his position.

"Play chess, Avery?" asked Henry, suddenly.

"A bit. At least, I did before I came here. Not much chance at Beckfield."

"That's what I find. That's why I go to see Will Lockyer at Martindale every Friday. He's a good chap who bought his, as they say, in World War One. Plays a grand game of chess, though."

Avery looked interested. Here was a new side to old Uncle Humbug, and one he hadn't anticipated.

"Your one-time batman? No, of course not." The Old Man couldn't have been more than a schoolboy during that war.

"Met him through the British Legion," explained Henry. "Chap there asked if I could find a fellow to give Lockyer an occasional game—this was about five years ago. The man who used to play with him had died, and take it by and large Beckfield's like everywhere else, has more use for TV and the pools than chess." And he added with his faint grin, "Bit of a snip for me."

This habit of his of dropping into contemporary slang always took Avery unaware.

"Any evenings Mr. Smith can spare you," Henry went on.

Avery jumped up. "We get out here. Yes, rather, Uncle Henry. We must fix it up."

The bus was stopped by lights. Henry, perfectly unflustered, inquired, "Who taught you? Or were you born knowing?"

"Chess? A chap called Russik."

Even Henry was taken by surprise. "Not . . . ?"

"That's right. Oh, you get all sorts in the camps." He added dispassionately, "He died out there just before I came back."

A difficult fellow, reflected Henry, with the knack of

making you seem in the wrong. Wouldn't surprise him to know that Richard and Charles had said good-bye with a sense of relief, one of those rare occasions when duty and desire ran together as smoothly as a four-in-hand.

Henry travelled another twenty minutes before it was time for him also to alight. Gathering up his armful of papers, slapping his pocket to make sure he had brought the cigarettes, he got out, crossed the common with its pond and its sleeping dog, and turned into a lane of small narrow houses. Here he swung open a gate and walked up a little flagged path. There was no need for him to ring the bell. Martha, half-distraught with Will's premonitions of disaster, was watching from the window of the sick man's room. She came hurrying down.

"How is he, Mrs. Lockyer?" asked Henry. He detached two or three of the papers and dropped them on the old wooden chest. They were for her, promising a delightful week-end when Will was deep in his magazines and didn't want to be interrupted.

The sick man had been watching anxiously from his bed that was drawn up beside the window. He greeted Henry with guarded enthusiasm. Martha was distressed, fearful that Mr. Browne would misinterpret. But if Henry noticed anything, and no one could ever be sure how much he did see, he gave no sign. As usual, the miracle was accomplished. Within five minutes Will was a changed man.

"And nothing special said," Martha marvelled to the friend from the end cottage with whom she spent this cherished hour of liberty. "Just a cigarette and a question —shall we degut GATT or regut GATT or something of the kind, and Will's away at once."

When they had talked some time Will got out the chess board, and when Martha came in an hour later with two glasses of beer on a tray they were hard at it.

"Wait a minute, Martha," said her husband in absorbed tones. "According to Russik it's white to play and check in two moves. But I don't see . . ."

"Russik!" thought Henry. Queer to hear the name

twice within the hour. He never drank beer in any house but this, but he drained his half pint as though he liked it before he stood up and shook hands. Martha walked with him to the door.

"He'll be as right as rain now," said she gratefully. "There's a programme on the TV to-night he's been looking forward to."

She stood there, big and smiling and rosy, concealing all her troubles behind her quiet face.

"And now," reflected Henry, walking away, "for the crux of the evening. Now for Stella."

Stella Foster heard the swing of the little iron gate and came into the hall. Henry had a key but he never used it, a small gesture of delicacy that she appreciated. It made her feel the house was hers and he was the guest, which was what he had in mind. The small change of courtesy came easy to him.

"Good evening, my darling." He gave the endearment no more value than the penny you throw to the organ-grinder's monkey or the cripple with the matches. "A new dress?"

He put his stick and raincoat down on the fake oak chest in the hall; he wasn't responsible for the house's furniture, but Stella didn't seem to mind the fumed oak, the brass warming-pan, the framed lithographs. He wondered if she even saw them.

She watched him sink into his usual chair and, standing behind him so that she could watch his face in the long mirror on the opposite wall, she said, "I've got some news for you, Henry."

"Then we can surprise each other," returned Henry cordially. "You begin."

She opened the sideboard and took out the whisky she never drank herself.

"Say when."

"My darling (he'd never call Beverley my darling) you must know my tastes after so long."

She handed him the glass. "It's about Sydney."

" Your husband? " He set the glass down so that the liquid splashed on to the table's surface. She noted that, thinking, " He's nervous. I wonder why. Henry's never clumsy." Henry went on with his usual smoothness, " He's not suddenly appeared, like Enoch Arden? "

She didn't know who Enoch Arden was. Except for film magazines, she didn't read.

" No. He's dead."

Henry took up his glass. " What an ungracious chap he sounds. Not a squeak out of him for five years, and then he breaks the silence to let you know he's dead."

" Not him. The police."

Henry put the glass down again, very carefully. " Why the police? And how did they know where to find you? "

" I suppose Sydney told them."

He said slowly, " My darling, he hasn't been pestering you all this time, and you've kept it to yourself? "

" He wrote once or twice."

" For money? Why didn't you tell me? "

" Why should you be bothered? "

" Blackmail. You ought to have told me, Stella. He had no right . . ."

" He was my husband."

" He wasn't supporting you."

" No. But if he'd asked me to go back to him he'd have been within his rights."

" As a lawyer," Henry began, and she broke in, " Is that what you are? You never told me."

" As a lawyer would assure you," continued Henry, steadily, " a man in his position can't make claims. How did he die? "

" It was a car accident. They said he was drunk and ran into a fence. I went to the hospital, but it was too late. He was dead. He was buried yesterday," she added.

If Henry was shocked by her callousness, he didn't show it. Stella waited for his comments, but when none came she went on, " This changes everything, doesn't it? It would be hypocrisy to pretend I'm sorry. I hadn't set eyes on him for years. And I'll tell you something else,

Henry. I shan't be sorry to leave this house either. I don't like prying neighbours and that's a fact. That woman opposite lives in her front window—I don't believe she ever sleeps. And that Miss Mence next door —I think she's out of her mind—hasn't enough business of her own to interest her, so must poke her nose into other people's."

" I never realised you weren't happy here," said Henry, surprised. " Fortunately we only have the house on a monthly tenancy. We'll give notice right away. Where did you think of going? "

She came round at last and seated herself opposite him. " It all depends. Henry, I want to be married."

He thought, " So she can still surprise me." It was a pity she hadn't been more evasive in the past; she hadn't given him cause for astonishment in an age. He thought that was probably the way of it in dozens of marriages that came to grief. Not hate, not resentment even, just weariness and boredom, the knowledge that to-day would be like yesterday and to-morrow the same as to-day. He knew now that she bored him to tears.

" My darling, you never breathed a hint. How secretive you are."

" It wasn't any use before. You see, I was brought up to believe marriage was for always. And then I don't like the idea of divorce courts and judges asking questions about your private life. But now Sydney's dead and everything's all right."

" I hope you'll be happy," he said. Something was going wrong with the conversation; he wasn't quite sure what it was. She was altogether too calm. A woman who's been kept by a man for five years should surely experience a little embarrassment at telling him she's proposing to drop him overboard and marry someone else. And then he knew what she meant and wondered how he could have been such a fool that he didn't understand from the start. His own heart felt like a bit of granite in his breast.

She said, " Oh, Henry, it's too late for fencing. It's you I want to marry. How could you have thought there would be anyone else? "

He lay back very gently, like a man who's had a bad shaking and isn't sure yet if any bones are broken.

" My darling, let's be realistic about this. You know there's never been any thought of marriage between us."

" We couldn't. There was Sydney."

" We could have disposed of Sydney without much difficulty if that was how we'd wanted it. You've admitted you could have got a divorce . . ."

He stopped again. Of course she couldn't have got a divorce. He should have realised that. No doubt she and Sydney had arranged to go their own ways. He thought, " If it had been Beverley and she were married and couldn't cut free, I'd take her to live with me, change her name by deed poll, brave the whole community and to hell with Beckfield, sooner than lose her." Of course, he had never dreamed of marrying Stella.

Stella folded her hands in the lap of the green dress that threw a greenish shade on her pale hair. She looked like a princess from under the sea till you saw the lines in the thin face, the taut mouth. Still, even now she had something that would always call men, as once it had called him.

" You've always taken for granted that whatever you thought was what we both wanted," she told him quietly. " Of course, I've thought of marriage. Being a kept woman isn't an easy life."

He couldn't resist the reflection that it would be hard to find one that made fewer demands.

" Look, my darling," he said persuasively. " Let's be frank over this. We were a bit in love, we had a good time, we've been friends since, but the best of things come to an end. If we'd thought this would be a permanent relationship we'd have taken steps to acknowledge it to the world. In a way, part of its charm has been its impermanence."

" You needn't go on, Henry," she said, still in that

voice of appalling gentleness. " I understand you, I always have. You want to put an end to things."

" You make it sound so violent," murmured Henry. " Things come to an end quite naturally; you can't have spring all the year round. Our season is drawing to its close, and my darling, we both know it."

" I suppose the truth is you want to marry someone else," said Stella baldly, too sick with pain to be wise.

Henry stiffened inwardly, but he kept his voice unchanged as he replied, " As to that, if I'm not to die an old bachelor I can't afford to lose any more time."

" Someone special? " insisted Stella, ruthless as the dentist's drill and to him at this moment about as desirable.

" I think, my darling, when we've parted, my future is my own concern."

" I suppose it's some girl half your age."

" Middle-aged men usually marry women young enough to be their daughters," Henry agreed suavely. " There would be very little sense else."

" Because of the children. Did it ever occur to you that I should have liked children? "

" No," said Henry, bluntly, " it didn't. You've always told me you were thankful you had no encumbrances— your word, my darling, not mine."

" I didn't want Sydney's children without Sydney, that's common sense. Children need two parents in their own home. I know. I came from a broken home myself."

It seemed to Henry this conversation could go on for ever, she insisting and he denying; and he was almost at the end of his endurance.

" Stella, my dear," he said, " it's no good. There's no question of marriage between us and never has been. Nor is there any question of your being an innocent young girl betrayed by an elderly roué. You were twenty-eight when I met you, with four years of married life behind you. We never thought of it as a permanent arrangement, and you can't say I've been tyrannical. You've had all the freedom you've wanted . . ."

"And now I don't want it any more. How simple life must be to people like you, Henry. Like snakes, shedding each skin as soon as it becomes uncomfortable. Only I'm not just another skin. I'm me, Stella Foster, a person with rights and feelings. Oh, I quite understand your position. You've met this girl and she's young and fresh and men are always young enough to make a new start. Have you told her anything about me?"

"I've told you," said Henry patiently, "I don't propose to discuss my private life."

Calmly Stella dropped the match into the petrol pool. "That's why you've never told me your real name, isn't it?" she suggested. "'They call me Mr. Browne,' you said. 'Henry to you, my darling.' And I'm such a fool I've only realised quite recently it was as phony as the address that went with it. I suppose you didn't want me to find out who you really are."

"Just Henry Browne," asserted Henry, steadily. "Don't you like it that way? You're the only woman in *his* life."

"And now he's conveniently going to die? But *I* can't die just to please him. Had you thought of that, Henry? You think of so much. The address in Hive Street—when I heard about Sydney I wrote to you, and when you didn't answer I came to see you. Well, you know what I found."

"A little tobacconist's shop," Henry agreed, "with an accommodation address for correspondence."

"Yes. I went in and asked if Mr. Browne had been in that day. The man behind the counter—were you quite careful enough about him, Henry? I think blackmail might be his middle name—said 'What Mr. Browne?' I explained that I'd written him a letter, but I'd changed my mind and wanted to get it back. He said he couldn't part with any letters except to their addressees. I asked him if people called for their post, or if he re-addressed it. He said, 'It's all according.' He's like you, Henry. He knows all the answers. You should be careful."

"An admirably discreet middle-man," Henry agreed.

He put down his glass and stood up. "I'm sorry you've been to so much trouble, my darling. Our delightful relationship has survived five years because we've each respected the other's privacy, or so I supposed. It's a pity we must end on a jarring note, but perhaps presently you will be able to think more kindly of me."

"What an optimist you are, Henry. In another minute you'll be telling me you hoped I'd feel just the same about it as you do."

Her mouth, very lightly painted, curved into a deprecatory smile.

"You mustn't expect too much," she reproached him. "You know quite well every woman falls in love with you on sight, and, though I'm sure they're all very accommodating, you can't expect them to fall out of love the minute you do. The plain truth is, I'm still in love with you. You can't say I've made trouble for you all these years. I've been an exemplary mistress, now is my chance to show you I can be an exemplary wife. But," here her voice hardened, "if you don't mean to give me the chance, at least I'll see to it that you don't marry anyone else."

"My dear Stella." He sounded a shade impatient. "Now we're becoming absurd. This isn't a melodrama——" His voice halted abruptly; urbanity changed to blank astonishment. Stella began to laugh.

"Are you sure, Henry? Quite, quite sure?"

He was frowning. "What's that thing in your hand?" he demanded. "And in Heaven's name, how did you get hold of it? Put it away, there's a good girl. We don't want an accident."

Stella was smiling, a smile that looked as though it were painted on her face.

"I should think you could see what it is, and it belonged to Sydney. When we were first married we lived in a very wild place almost a wood, you could say, and there were tramps. Sydney sometimes had to be away at night on the firm's business, so he got this and he taught me to use it."

27

" Very rash of him, my darling," suggested Henry. " What was wrong with a dog? "

" He did get a dog, but it ran away. Anyway, I never cared particularly for dogs, and this was the kind that looks like a wolf. I used to think—suppose it has a sudden wild fit when I'm here alone, I could scream my head off and no one would hear. I really felt more comfortable with a revolver."

" How often have you fired it? " asked Henry.

" I've never shot anyone, if that's what you mean, but I'm quite a good shot, or used to be. Sydney taught me, he said I was a credit to him. When he went away he left it behind. I suppose he'd forgotten all about it."

" Have you got a licence? " Henry asked.

" No. Do I need one? For a gun I've never used? How silly! "

" If you're thinking of using it now you may find the police asking awkward questions. You'd better give it to me, Stella." He held out his hand.

" You don't believe I'd use it, do you? " Stella taunted him.

" My darling, it's precisely because I fear you may that I'm anxious to get it into my own possession."

" I think I'll keep it just the same. About the licence— I think it would be a mistake to call anyone's attention to it just now. They might even take it away from me."

" And you're anxious to keep it."

" You never know when it might come in useful."

" I can't believe you intend to commit suicide, so I'm driven to suppose you intend, in certain circumstances, to turn it on me. How would that help you? "

" It would be the simplest thing for all of us. You're a natural trouble-maker, Henry, whether you mean it or not. I don't suppose I'm the first woman whose heart you've proposed to break." She saw his instinctive wincing away from the stereotyped phrase, and her face hardened. " But don't think you've won. I can't shoot you, my fingers would fall from the trigger, but I warn you of this. If ever you take that girl to church, whoever she may be, and I shall find out her name, don't ask me how, you'll find me waiting outside with this." She flourished the revolver in his direction. " At that range I couldn't miss. And no one can prevent spectators crowding round a church door. Why, Henry, you've turned as white as a sheet. I believe for the first time you realise I'm not play-acting. And, of course, it's true. I mean every word I say."

Henry had faced her calmly enough when the danger had threatened only his own life, but that Beverley, Beverley the incomparable, the cherished, the meaning of life and the colour of the new day, now that she stood in mortal danger, he could feel his heart churning in his breast. It seemed as though it might smash through the delicate cage of his ribs and flounder like some living thing in the little space between them. The room had been dimly lit on his arrival, what Stella called an intimate illumination. Now it seemed full of darkness, and her voice came to him out of that darkness.

" Don't think this is hysteria, Henry. I've been thinking ever since I realised there was someone else. Oh, how smug you are! " she burst out in a fresh access of fury. " Thinking that this is the real thing at last and all the rest just time-fillers, and me one of them. But someone should have warned you not to play with fire, Henry, because if you do you get burned. And remember, I meant all that. So, if you go ahead with this marriage, you'll be accessory before the fact. Apart from anything else, Henry, it wouldn't do *you* any good. You'd be like Ishmael, with every man's hand against you. I know you're very sure of yourself, I expect you have quantities of friends who think what a good fellow he is, what good company, how amusing, but you'd be surprised how quickly they'd change when the facts came out. You wouldn't have anyone left, not even me. Don't say anything more now, Henry. You've had a shock. Go home and think over what I've said. I'm sure you'll see reason. And I don't really think you'd be very good as a husband to a young wife. She'd make demands, the sort I've never made. And youth should go with youth. You don't have to do anything drastic, just keep away from her—you're not actually engaged, are you? Well, you couldn't very well be with us the way we are. Did you really come this evening to break everything off, so neat, so tidy? It's for your own good as well as mine . . ."

Henry stood up. He had allowed her to run on because he was, as she said, stunned by the situation. Now, putting out his hand, he said, " Give me that thing, Stella. You must be out of your mind . . ."

" Not yet. Not till I've fired it. Then I could claim temporary insanity. No, don't try and take it from me. It might go off."

She reminded him of Coleridge's Christabel, standing there so straight and malign.

Each eye shrank up to a serpent's eye . . .

" You'd best be getting along, Henry, and think things over," she advised him, paying no heed to his demand. " But don't think I don't mean what I said. So long as I live you shan't marry anyone else."

CHAPTER III

AFTERWARDS IT seemed to Henry he must have had some sort of a mental black-out, for when he realised what he was doing he found he was out of the house and walking blindly down the road, with the echo of the clanging gate ringing in his ears. He had no notion where he was going or what he intended to do, but he knew he would fight for his love with an ardour that had never fired him for any other cause. He had been too young to enlist in the First World War, and he had never sympathised with his brother, Christopher, intervening in a fight not his own. What would the English think if a Spanish republican force landed on their shores to take part in a civil war? Well, that point at least didn't arise. It took the conceited English to think up the Crusades, reflected Henry, turning into the High Street and marching along as if he intended to reach the end of the world. After a while a bus came past, and he hailed it. He had no notion where it went, but he swung himself aboard and offered half a crown saying, "All the way." The bus ran on for a long time, leaving houses and village greens behind it till, as the shadows deepened, they were traversing a space of empty fields and distant cottages, their walls patched with squares of gold light. Eventually they stopped for good outside an inn called The Running Dog. There were only two passengers left now, and the other turned to cross the road and disappear down a lane. Henry pushed into the lighted bar of the inn and found himself in a crowd of men, none of whom paid the smallest attention to his arrival. He must, therefore, look comparatively normal, not the madman he felt himself to be. He went to the bar and bought a large whisky that he carried to a small table in the corner. He had, scarcely knowing what he did, picked up a newspaper left in the bus by one of the other travellers, and that alone showed he wasn't himself, because newspapers left in buses are natural perquisite of the conductor. He unfolded it and held it up, not seeing a word. All round him the buzz of conversation continued unabated. The door swung open with a creak as newcomers arrived, some to be welcomed by those already on the premises, others, like himself, buying a drink and moving off with it alone. The only voice he heard now was Stella's.

" I promise you, Henry, so long as I live you won't marry this girl."

The words came ringing back in his ears like the clapper of a bell. *So long as I live . . . so long as I live . . .*

It must have been then that the idea of murder first slid into his mind.

Murder! A strange, a hideous word, and one to which he was unaccustomed. Greatorex was an old-fashioned firm, very respectable and demure. It didn't handle violent and unseemly crimes like homicide, Richard and Charles even looked down their aristocratic noses at divorce.

" Do they think they're magicians that they can turn back the clock? " Avery had wondered. " Gentlemen, that's what they call themselves, and don't understand there's no room for their kind of gentleman in the savage society in which we're living to-day. Men want lawyers because they find themselves in a jam and want to be helped out of it."

The Greatorex Brothers were like those diehards who cry loyally, " Motors? Horrible stinking machines. Give us that noble beast, the horse," conveniently forgetting that horses have natural functions, and the smell of petrol isn't the only smell that can offend the susceptibilities.

" Murder! " repeated Henry to himself, feeling like a man in a nightmare. He must have spoken aloud for a barman, materialising from nowhere, stopped inquiringly by his table. Hurriedly he ordered another whisky-and-soda. It was clear that the man had no idea who he was, which went to show what very small fry Greatorexes were once they were outside their own orbit. The drink arrived and he put down some money and picked up the glass. And all the time he saw nothing of his surroundings, couldn't have recognised the fellow who served him, if he met him face to face next morning. His mind gave him a stream of images ranging from Stella, always with the gun in her hand, the gun that, he knew without any doubt at all, she would not hesitate to use, to Beverley with her candid grey eyes, and heart-shaped face, and the voice that was like the music of angels, Beverley who, in short, he loved better than his own life. It wouldn't be murder, he reflected, but suicide by proxy. He'd heard a man say once that the law was too narrow in its judgments. Some men virtually slew themselves, though theirs may not be the hand to strike the blow, pour the poison, set the trap. They left the adversary no other way. To abandon all hopes of Beverley and to accept Stella's terms never even passed through his mind. Beverley and he were the world, and woe betide whoever attempted to separate them. He was really mad to-night, seeing nothing in perspective, a stranger to the cool Henry Greatorex that Beckfield knew, telling himself that, if harm came to Stella, she would have invited it as surely as if she had put the revolver to her head and pressed the trigger.

Presently he marched out of The Running Dog and began to walk in the direction of Beckfield. Nobody paid any attention to him or realised that they had just been forsaken by a man with murder in his heart.

After Henry had departed, saying no word, simply taking up his hat and raincoat and leaving her, as though she had dissolved into a drift of dust, Stella laid the gun aside and began to shake as though she had an ague. Like Henry, she was crazy with love; neither could have seen sense, each believed himself perfectly justified in the course he proposed. After a long time the loneliness of the house was like a threat; the shadows about her stirred, the place seemed full of eyes watching, feet stirring, hands stretching from dim corners. She pulled a coat over her shoulders and, without pausing for bag or gloves, in her turn let herself out of the house. Like Henry again, she had no notion where she was going, just let her feet take her where they would. If she encountered any passers-by, if they turned to stare at her shocked and stricken face, she was oblivious to them. She saw windows curtained against the curious gaze, sometimes she heard footsteps, but they were like steps heard in a dream, having no substance, while for any interest she took in her surroundings, every house she passed might have been blind. After some time she reached a big corner building, with lights blazing in all the windows, and, still like someone under a spell, she pushed open the door and walked in. She found herself in a large cheerful well-lighted room, with a bar at one end and a number of small tables, most of them occupied, covering the floor space. She espied one vacant table at the far end of the room, and, still numb, she moved over and seated herself. She wasn't aware that, within a few moments of her arrival, the eyes of practically every man in the room had turned in her direction. There was about her to-night something so fey, so strange and compelling that, having once looked, they seemed unable to return their gaze. If Stella had been able to think of anyone but Henry she might have remembered that this was precisely the effect she had had on Sydney at their first meeting. And not on Sydney alone. But Sydney and every other man in the world was dead to her to-night. She only remembered that Henry hadn't been swept off his feet. Oh, he had been attracted, charmed, presently even a little in love, but never out of control. He had been a considerate and graceful lover, treating love like some delightful pet to whom you give a home. But love, thought demented Stella, was more like a jungle brute. If Sydney had threatened him with something far less lethal than a revolver he would have withdrawn gracefully. But for this strange girl he was prepared to take any risk. There they were then, two creatures caught in a trap, and surely, surely one of them must die.

When the waiter came to her table she asked for brandy and drank it as though it were water when it was brought. Business in the bar was brisk at this hour; in a room on the left, through swing doors, people were dining, although it was now almost nine o'clock. Those at the tables were those who dined at home and came here afterwards for a bit of social life. Up at the bar a stout man in regrettably bright brown suiting was talking cheerfully to his neighbours. Facing him was a long mirror in which was reflected all the life of the room. He saw the woman enter, saw the immediate reaction of practically every man on the premises. For himself, he recognised something that was perhaps less apparent to them, that here was a woman almost beside herself with distress. " I'd as soon tangle with a tiger-cat as get across that one," was his characteristic reflection.

He watched her drain the brandy and order a second with scarcely a moment's pause. The waiter was very busy this evening and he hadn't asked for payment for the first drink when he brought it, but when he deposited the second and she treated it in precisely the same manner, he waited by the table, murmuring the price of the two doubles. In the glass the big red-faced man (Crook's the name, Arthur Crook of 123 Bloomsbury Street, my clients are always innocent and we work all round the clock, was his customary manner of introduction) watching closely, saw her vague, unseeing glance from one empty chair to the other, saw her dig her hands into the pockets of her coat and bring them out empty, and then shake her head, all in the same demented fashion. It was clear that she hadn't any money and didn't appreciate the awkwardness of her situation.

" Not known here," decided Crook. " No money and couldn't care less."

The waiter moved off through the swing doors. " Gone to fetch the manager," decided Crook. In the eyes of one

35

or two drinkers who, like himself, were unaccompanied, he saw a predatory gleam. Before any of them could move, he had detached himself from the bar, and, with no impression of haste, had reached her table and was pulling out one of the empty chairs.

The woman turned her head; she didn't seem surprised to see him. He got the impression she was beyond surprise or any normal emotion. Taken the knock was his old-fashioned way of phrasing it. He glanced at her hand; she still wore Sydney Foster's wedding ring, and it occurred to him that she might be suddenly widowed. Only surely she would have put on something less noticeable than that dress of jade green wool. For the same reason, he did not think she had lost a beloved child in an accident or just come from a death bed. No, it was sly old Dan Cupid doing his stuff as usual. Someone had stood her up or she had learned that her lover was married and did not want to break with his wife or something of the kind. He wasn't one for the dames, he would have told you, was no more moved by her feminine qualities than if she had been a lady baboon, but he knew trouble when he saw it and he had not grown up in the gentlemanly *milieu* that waits for an introduction before it speaks.

Out of the corner of his eye he saw the swing doors reopening. The dark young waiter came back followed by the manager. It wasn't the sort of place where they'd want trouble. They would stand the loss of a couple of double brandies, and well they could afford to, but she would probably be asked quite politely to leave.

" Have this one on me, sugar," said Crook. " Yes, it's O.K. I've been led up the garden path myself in my time, and I never was a great one for horticulture."

Glancing up, as the two men reached her table, he said, " Same again for me and the young lady at the bar knows what that is, and this lady will take . . ."

She looked at him doubtfully; he was pretty sure she didn't really see him, was just aware of someone in the chair beside her. I could be a gorilla or a baby elephant and she wouldn't know the difference, he reflected. "How about a nice cup of coffee—hot and black?" he suggested.

"Yes, thank you."

If he had suggested prussic acid it would probably have been all the same and most likely a lot more good to her. The manager, giving the impression that he had come in to have a word with some of the regulars, walked past with a bright "Good evening," and stopped a couple of tables up. The waiter went off to fetch the order and Crook said, "Take my tip and have a bite to eat when the coffee comes. They do you a handsome ham sandwich here."

Still she said nothing, so he continued more robustly, "Waiting for the watched pot, sugar? Take the advice of the man who knows, it's always a waste of time."

She asked curiously, "Have you ever killed anyone?"

"Only indirectly," said Crook. "I mean, getting my chap out of quod and somebody else's chap in. Oh, and the war, of course." He meant the 1914 war; he had spent the whole of the second one in London, dodging the bombs. "If you're asking for my advice," he went on, "not that I expect you to take it—dames never do— lay off murder. It don't pay."

She seemed to see him for the first time and her green eyes flew open.

"I know," said Crook. "You're thinking I look like Mr. Fair-and-Square. Fact is, I started wearing this shade of brown before I knew better, and now it's like a uniform, I can't shed it till I retire."

She said, "Who are you?"

Crook put his hand in his pocket and brought out a card. "Crook's the name, Arthur Crook. Here's my address."

She glanced at it, not much interested. "Oh— London."

"Well, don't say it like that," Crook adjured her. "There's no better place in the world, and, to tell you the truth, I'm surprised to find myself in this little one-horse show. But I came down to get some information about a client, and to-morrow morning you won't see me for dust."

The beer came and the coffee, and Crook ordered a couple of ham sandwiches.

"Why did you come over here?" asked Stella, in so simple a tone the question was robbed of any offensive taint.

"I thought maybe you'd forgotten your handbag. That could happen to anyone."

"Yes. I came out in a hurry." She looked round her. "What is this place?"

"A classy joint called the Nell Gwynn. Never been here before?"

She shook her head. "I don't live near here. I just came in when I saw the lights."

"And I dare say if it had been the river you'd have walked into that. Take my tip, sugar, never make any decisions after 2 p.m. Things always look different in the morning."

"People tell you that, but it isn't true. Everything will be just the same to-morrow."

"I didn't say it 'ud *be* different. I only said it 'ud *look* different." He took his change from the waiter and handed some of it back for service. "Living alone?" he went on.

He felt her stiffen. "Why?"

"I'm not makin' a pass at you, sugar. My romantic days are done. Only solitude does queer things to people. You take a couple of aspirins and get a nice night's sleep. No one's worth losing your beauty sleep for. Only —don't lose count and take the whole bottle."

The swing doors to the dining-room parted again and three people came out, a man and two women. The man was a handsome well-set-up fellow of about fifty, with chestnut hair only slightly marked with grey, and an arresting face. My sort of chap, reflected Crook. Knows what he wants and don't mind what he pays for it. A reckless type and difficult, but better, in Crook's opinion, than the man who knows what he wants and intends to have it, but raises no objection to some other fellow footing the bill. The women were his wife and, from the resemblance between the two women, the wife's sister. They were a jolly, good-looking pair, and the one wearing a wedding-ring was well dressed in a solid, unimaginative way. Her fur coat was good, her crocodile bag the real thing. Prosperous business crowd, decided Crook, not usually much good to him, but probably up to all the tricks. The Commissioners of Inland Revenue would have a ding-dong fight to get a ha'penny more than their due, and the chap was more likely to bypass them. A nice chap, thought Crook, a private enterpriser, a man who knew Providence had given him two feet in order to preserve his balance, and who did so perserve it. They had clearly all dined well and now they settled themselves at a table not far off for a final round.

Crook swept the crumbs of his ham sandwich off a waistcoat as plumply rounded as a robin's breast and stood up.

" Nice knowing you, sugar," he said. " Keep this, you might want it some time."

He gave her the card and she pushed it carelessly into the pocket of her coat.

"And if temptation gets too strong," he said, " and it comes to a fatal end, remember, I only act for the innocent and I'm always open to an offer."

She lifted those strange green eyes and he thought, well, a few centuries ago you would have been burnt at the stake. He wasn't surprised at the attention she had attracted. She was like a magnet. The latest-comer had already slewed his eyes in her direction, in spite of the presence of his wife and sister-in-law.

" You mean, if I did kill someone . . ."

Crook caught her arm with his leg-of-mutton hand. "Now hold it, sugar. Remember, the tongue is a little member, but it is set on fire of hell. No names, no pack-drill. I mean, my clients are always innocent or they wouldn't be my clients. Get me? "

She dropped her eyes and folded her long hands on her lap. Crook felt a little uncomfortable. He didn't quite know what to make of her. She was a million miles removed from the Rum Old Girls who were his cup of tea, but she wasn't a youngster like the central figures of his last two murder cases. He had a horrid feeling that this might turn into murder and he might find himself involved, and you would only need to put this woman in the box to see Justice slink off with its tail between its legs. Women jurors—Guilty as hell. Men—Justifiable homicide. That was how he read it, and he was not often wrong about hunches of this kind.

"Thank you for the drinks and the sandwich," she said. "I'll be going back soon."

"Sure you're fit to drive?" Not that he intended to offer to take her home. No sense sticking your neck out too far.

"I haven't got a car. There'll be a bus or something."

He thought grimly it was more likely to be something. He put his hand in his pocket and laid half a crown on the table.

"Cab fare," he explained. "That's O.K., sugar. You can buy me one next time."

He walked back to the bar and ordered another pint. "Warm in here," he offered.

The man to whom he had been talking grinned. "You're a fast worker," he remarked.

But if that was true Crook wasn't the only one in the bar that night. The man with chestnut hair couldn't keep his eyes off the woman—he hadn't even got her name, though later everyone was to know it. His wife said something, laughing gently, and putting her hand on his arm. The man turned abruptly away. There was no laughter in his eyes, he looked confused.

"Gosh, Maggie!" thought Crook. "He's sold right up the river."

He had seen that look on a man's face before. It meant that if murder was the only way to get what he wanted, well, murder it must be. Not, of course, that he thought

of murder in this connection, which shows that even the
best of us can be wrong on occasions. It was going to be
Murder with a capital M over all the press and not so
far ahead at that.

The second time the wife attempted to distract her
husband's attention she, too, had ceased to smile, and a
few minutes later the trio rose and left the bar. They
seemed pretty well known here. The manager, who was
hovering, ran forward to say he hoped he would see them
next Friday as usual. Crook heaved a sigh of relief. He
didn't mind rough houses, except when he was off duty.
He had plenty of trouble between Brandon Street where
he lived and Bloomsbury Street where he worked. Like
most Londoners, he expected to find peace in the country,
and he visited it too seldom for him to realise the absurdity
of his expectation. He had just had one for the road and
was leaving the bar when he saw a man hurrying across the
street. It was the fellow with the chestnut hair, and he
pushed past Crook as though he did not even see him.
Well, reflected the little cockney lawyer, Green Eyes
isn't the only one who has taken the knock. He climbed
into the Old Superb, his recently acquired twenty-year-old
Rolls, with the high body and the bright yellow coach-
work, and sat for a moment at the wheel. Before he had
put her into gear the door of the bar swung open once
more and out came Coppernob with Green Eyes in tow.
The light of a street lamp fell clear on their faces. Hers
was still numb, she had been knocked off her balance
and hadn't straightened out yet, his was intense and
burning. Crook told himself he could feel the heat across
the width of the road. He didn't really believe in the
miracle of love at first sight, and he didn't imagine he
was seeing it now, but he did believe in witchcraft and
that was what he had seen to-night. The woman,
without so much as lifting her eyes, had put a spell on the
man that had blinded him to good sense, good feeling
and his own interests. What he hoped to get from these
shock tactics was anyone's guess. He didn't look the
sort of fellow to make a fool of himself easily, yet he

had shaken off both his female encumbrances and come beetling back. Left a pair of gloves or pretended to, no doubt, though how he was going to explain to his wife that it took him an hour or more to find them was his headache. He had a handsome grey Bentley at the kerb, and he handed Green Eyes in. Going to take her home, obviously; and make another date? Crook did not know. Anyhow, it was not his affair, or so he thought. He did not guess that before long he was going to be in it up to the neck.

When the grey car stopped outside Stella Foster's house it was seen by the Fanshawes opposite. Mrs. Fanshawe spent half her life at the window.

" She's come back," she told her sister, who was spending a few weeks with them, between jobs. " *Another man*. I call it disgraceful. This is supposed to be a respectable neighbourhood."

" Why don't you send her a letter? " asked the friend. " No need to sign it."

" I might at that," agreed Mrs. Fanshawe.

Mr. Fanshawe, who spent most of his leisure reading and doing crosswords, except when he was at the Coach and Horses, looked up.

" Don't you put nothing on paper, Emily," he warned her. " Most of the trouble of the world comes from putting things into writing."

He thought with a sigh of a certain letter he had written thirty years ago, having no more sense than most young chaps of his age, and look at the consequences. Nag, nag, nag, morning, noon and night. He could hardly go to the public without her tagging along and meeting him as he came home. " Why don't you come along o' me and have a drink like a Christian? " he would say, but she did not hold with the drink, and indeed, if she had accepted, there would be his last stronghold stormed. All the same, he didn't want her making trouble with letters to the woman across the road, whose life was her own and, so long as she did not make trouble for the neighbours, was no concern of theirs. She was not his fancy—he had had a scunner with one woman, and, like Crook, did not want to be tangled up with any other—but it was no affair of theirs how she spent her time, and there was a thing no woman had ever heard of seemingly, called libel, and, under the archaic British laws, men were still responsible for their wives, and any bits and bobs of cash he had he wanted for transactions at the local, not for damages for loss of character. So, " You lay off the pen, Emily," he said. " She don't bother you."

" I was brought up in a God-fearing home," said Emily, severely. " That's the second man she's had in her house to-night."

" Perhaps they're her brothers," said the henpecked husband, feebly.

" Brothers! Sometimes, Joe, I think you're right daft." He went back to his book. He might as well have saved his breath. Nothing he said made any difference.

CHAPTER IV

AFTER THE red-headed man who had given her his card had returned to the bar, Stella sat where she was in a daze of stupefaction that had enveloped her since Henry stormed out of her house. Nothing that had happened that evening seemed a part of reality. She had never intended in the first place to threaten him with the revolver, whose existence, indeed, she had forgotten for years. Clearing out some of the old stuff left behind by Sydney she had come upon it, and, having nothing particular to do, had amused herself by cleaning it, and had put it in a bureau drawer. Then, when Henry made his situation clear, out her hand had stolen and pulled the drawer wide, while the words she had not known she was going to speak had sprung to her lips. If she had thought of using the weapon at all she might have staged a big scene in which she shot first Henry and then herself, but she knew now, if she had not then, that she could never turn the weapon upon him. She had met Mr. Crook's advances with the same apathy as she turned to the second stranger who came thrusting through the swing-doors to stop at her table, looking like a madman, she thought now. He had besought her, not knowing her name or her circumstances, to come out with him some time, any time, now. Was she waiting for someone? Was she expected anywhere? Well, then, had she her own car? No? Then at least let her permit him to drive her home.

She was less startled by his violence, would have been less startled even if she had been in a normal mood, than most women, since she had suffered the same sense of unreasoning desire herself. And, moreover, had been the source of it before to-day. She had never been one to sit at home with a good book in the evening, time enough for that when you are old and men have stopped turning to look after you, and don't notice you, except the good-hearted ones who give up a seat in a bus or a train, and she loved colour and light and fun, the sound of life hurrying past like a river, rushing by houses and pubs and music halls, and taking all their reflections on its shining breast. She did not ask much, she thought, but she used to go round to the local of an evening, a good-class one, mind you, not one of these places like the Lord Derwent or the Exeter Grey, where betting slips passed all the time, and that, during the war, were hotbeds for black marketeers. No, a nice refined glass of whatever she fancied in the saloon bar—she wasn't daft enough to patronise the Ladies' Bar, that was for the old trots who hadn't got men to entertain them or were past attracting them—but it always worked out the same. Quite soon she would start recognising some of the regulars, and it was never long before someone was saying " What's yours? " and the evening settled down for her. Sometimes they walked back to the house in Hallet Street, now and again she would ask them in—just one for the road, she would say. Mostly it was just to talk and have a bit of fun, but occasionally, not often mark you, they stayed later; it was all according. It never seemed to her there was anything wrong about this. It was Nature and you weren't an old woman at thirty-three. As for Henry, she had no sense of disloyalty to him. It was not like being a wife, and he was not in love, would not boil over at the thought of her finding a bit of comfort in another man's arms. Until he met the unknown woman, and instantly transferred his frail allegiance, she had not realised how large a part of her life he represented; and the knowledge was like a poisoned dart in her breast.

When he walked out that evening she knew she had lost him for ever. She had left the little house because she could stay there no longer, she could as easily have remained in the heart of a fire. She had let Crook talk to her, pay for her drinks, leave his ridiculous half crown on the table, but none of it really registered. It was all part of some nightmare in which she could not even believe. And while she still sat there in a stupor, this second stranger came up and swept her off her feet and into his car, a handsome grey Bentley, she noticed without realising she had noticed it. When we're in the chips, Sydney used to say, we will have a Bentley. But long before that he had blown off. She let Gerald—he hadn't told her his other name or asked her for hers—come up with her, though she must have known how the evening would end. Ah, but it had not been Stella Foster who had gone through with the incident, only some shadow whom she watched with no feeling at all. After he had gone she had lain on the couch for a long time, staring at the drawn curtains, till it occurred to her that the fire was out and she was bitterly cold. She pulled herself to her feet and looked vaguely about her. The whisky she had never put away still stood on the little sideboard. She splashed some into a glass, she who never touched the stuff, loathing taste and smell alike, and drank it almost neat, choking as the fiery liquid ran down to warm her chilled body. Because there was nothing else to do, and this was a nightmare, and what happens in dreams is of no account, she refilled the glass. Now the daze was physical as well as mental. She was too tired to make up the fire, straighten the room, go upstairs. Pulling a rug about her, she slept.

In the morning, Crook had said, everything will look different. She had not believed him, but he was right. In the morning the street was just as it had been twenty-four hours before; there was nothing to show that a bomb had exploded and blown up her whole life. She tried to remember what Gerald looked like, but she could only recall the features of the man who'd given her his card and paid for her drinks and made her eat a ham sandwich. The half crown he had given her lay on the table; she supposed she had automatically pulled it out of her coat pocket, having nowhere else to put it, and dropped it there. Her recollection of what happened afterwards was as confused as ever. Gerald—would she ever see him again? It didn't matter, since for her he had no actual existence, nothing of last night touched the real Stella, or so she had believed then. But the clear morning light had no compassion. It compelled her to face the facts that misery and whisky, on top of the double brandies and the exhaustion that follows passion, had so successfully blunted until now. This morning the facts were as cruel as death. Henry had discarded her and she had permitted a stranger, for whom she had less than the normal feeling of friendliness and human desire, to bring her home and make love to her. And recalling this, she now found she could visualise no face but Henry's as he went away. Even Crook was no more than a shadow without features or name.

When she came into the hall she found a plain manilla envelope lying on the mat. It was unstamped and the letter it contained was unsigned. But the purport was perfectly clear if the language was somewhat unusual,

"We know about your men coming to see you you ought to be run out of the town on a rail it's a wonder you don't put out a red light we don't want harlots here"

it said with no punctuation and, naturally, no signature.

She stared at it stupidly; at first it did not seem really to matter, just a bit of spite from some jealous neighbour —old Miss Mence most likely. Poor old girl, everyone knew about her. Up the road with her little cairn dog that it would have been kinder to have put to sleep, reflected Stella, who had never heard of grammar and considered the sole use of words was to make one's meaning clear. Nosey old so-and-so, she muttered. She flung open the door in time to see Miss Mence coming up the road. She lived on Stella's farther side, would have to pass her gate. The little dog was moving slowly on three legs, the fourth held high.

On a sudden impulse Stella whirled to the gate.

"Didn't anyone ever tell you you can be sent to prison for slander?" she exclaimed. (It was libel of course, but

Stella did not know the difference.) "And the police don't like people that daren't sign their names to letters. If it comes to undesirable people, what about you with your yapping little dog that ought to have been put down years ago?"

Henry would have been shocked; this was a Stella he had never met, a Stella born of the twin devils of whisky and despair. Miss Mence's pale blue eyes widened, she fumbled for her key.

"I don't know what you're talking about, Mrs. Foster, really, I don't. I think you must be out of your mind." She looked at the little dog. "Come along, Sandy. He hurt his paw on a thorn," she explained.

"Not that you need worry," Stella continued, as reckless as her lover of the previous night. "I'm not staying here. Not likely. Now that my husband's dead . . ."

"Oh, dear!" Miss Mence was all of a flutter. "I—I'm very sorry. Was it very sudden?"

"A car accident. You can't be much more sudden. Well, now I'm going to get married, and naturally we shan't want to stay in this—this hen-coop."

"I hope you'll be very happy," faltered Miss Mence. "It must have been very trying—I mean——"

She was horrified to realise that what she really meant was that it must have been trying waiting for Mr. Foster to die, which wasn't at all the kind of sentiment a churchwoman should express.

"So, you see, Miss Mence," cried Stella, "you needn't waste any more paper and envelopes . . ."

"You're making a mistake." Miss Mence faced up to her, brown tweed hat slipping sideways on the plaited bunches of hair she wore over her long ears. "I have never written—why should I? We live next door."

"For all the communication we've ever had I might as well have been living in the Sahara," was Stella's grim retort. "But, if you have got anything you can't keep to yourself, come into my house and say it to my face."

Miss Mence scooped up the offended-looking Sandy,

who had a little black mask like a monkey, and smelt of dog, and lolloped off to her own house.

" What a thrill for her if I shoot a lover in my sitting-room," Stella thought, viciously. But even now she would not allow herself to believe it would come to that. " Be patient, keep your head and Henry will come back," she assured herself. He wasn't, after all, a young man, middle-aged passions burn themselves out.

In short, he must come back. Without him she was like someone struck blind, knowing that never again will he see colour or the light of the sun.

Nevertheless the following Friday came and went without any sign of Henry. Not that he stayed away from Martindale, he kept his usual appointment with Will Lockyer, but he did not, as usual, proceed to Hallett Street. Instead, he returned to Beckfield. All that evening Stella stayed indoors, waiting. He must come, she thought, if only to discover whether she had really meant what she said the previous week. From half-past seven, when he normally arrived, until eight o'clock she waited with growing feverishness. At eight o'clock she went up to her bedroom and sat behind the drawn curtains, watching every person who came down the road. By nine she knew he was not coming. At ten she locked the front door, but even then she did not go to bed. There was always a chance, she told herself, that he had been detained. There was no telephone so, of course, he couldn't ring her up. Soon after eleven Mrs. Fanshawe, peering through her curtains before calling it a day, saw the light go out.

" He's stood her up," she told her husband, gleefully.

Joe snored so loudly anyone would have known it wasn't genuine.

The following Friday Stella stayed in again, but now she did not really anticipate that Henry would come. Nor did he. Nevertheless, she tormented herself with every kind of hope. He was ill, had gone away, had written and by some mischance the letter had miscarried. But in her

49

heart she knew this was untrue. In five years Henry had never written. If he had had to put off a meeting he had sent a telegram which could not be traced. On the other evenings she went out the same as before. Each night saw her at the Coach and Horses or the Horn of Plenty, attracting men as she had always done, and not caring for one among them any more than if he had been a robot. But, robot-like herself, she went through all the motions, the slow smile, the narrowed eye, the upward lift of the head, not consciously alluring but as instinctive as an animal. She knew that, if she had any sense, all was not lost. Henry was gone; even if he gave up this girl he would never come back to her. But there were other men. There was Gerald Sumner, who had come storming back to the Nell Gwynn that first night because he couldn't stay away, and who had come again—and again. It had been no flash-in-the-pan affair for him, he was crazy for her, as crazy as Sydney had been, far more crazy than Henry, Henry whom she loved so jealousy that at the thought of his marrying another woman her heart fainted and her cheeks paled, and rage and despair shook her like bitter winds. He had not come back, and since she was sure his name was not Mr. Browne, she had no notion how to trace him. Two or three times she went to the street of the little tobacconist and hung about, casually looking in the windows, but he never put in an appearance.

In the meantime, Henry never had Stella out of his mind. Not that his office noticed any marked difference, but then he had always been careful to preserve privacy about his personal affairs. Only Addie Bainbridge detected a change, and agonised in her heart, knowing her own helplessness to do anything about it. She couldn't understand how it was that no one else seemed affected by the situation. Henry's intention of marrying Beverley if she would have him remained unchanged. But he did not underrate Stella. He was sure she would, if necessary, carry out her threat, and in the heart of this confusion he did not know which way to turn. Almost a month had passed since his last meeting with Stella when he reached a certain conclusion and decided to pay her another visit. It was a wet and wild Tuesday night, and after leaving the office it occurred to him that there might well be a communication awaiting him at the tobacconist's shop in Hive Street. So, before travelling into Martindale, he made his way thither. Casual as always, he strolled into the shop.

" Ah, Mr. Browne! " The sly little animal on the farther side of the counter gave him a knowing look, as he took a square pale-blue envelope out of a pigeon-hole and handed it across the counter. " This came yesterday."

Henry glanced at the envelope and saw Stella's familiar, sprawling hand, with the stamp set slightly askew. There was no mistaking her writing. He put it in his breast pocket and looked up to see Saunders's eye, as bright and black as a canary's, fixed on his face.

" Wouldn't your wife be interested to know what's inside that? " was what the look conveyed. Henry recalled Stella saying, " Are you sure you've been careful there? I should have said blackmail was his second name." And what an opportunity this sideline would give an unscrupulous little rat, assuming he could steam the letters open. Stella always sealed her envelopes with a dab of blue wax and stamped it with a little gold rose, that made Henry think of the pats of butter of his childhood, made up while you watched and stamped with a rose or a cottage or a cow. Sealing her letters was the kind of thing Stella did without being advised, not because she was afraid of them being opened, but because she thought it was *chic*. Henry had turned and was leaving the shop when Mr. Saunders recalled him.

" Oh, Mr. Browne—there was another letter come by an earlier post. Would that be for you, too? "

" Who else? " inquired Henry coolly, but he didn't like the sound of the man's voice, and this second envelope, that was now passed across to him, was not sealed. The writing was unfamiliar, careful but semi-literate; he had no notion whose it was, but he slipped the envelope casually into his pocket, aware of the insolent brown stare from the other side of the counter.

" You're a one-r, aren't you? " that stare demanded. " Two at the same time." For the handwriting on the second envelope was also obviously that of a woman.

Out of sight of the shop Henry slit open Stella's letter. It was very short and unsigned.

" I shall expect you this week," it read. " I meant everything I said, so you will be wise to come."

He tore the slip of paper into shreds, stuffing some into a convenient litter basket and letting the dreary wind blow away the rest. The note was on a par with the sudden production of the revolver, melodrama to the penultimate degree. The final degree, of course, would be when she really brought the weapon into play, and in order to prevent the possibility of this he was proposing to visit her to-night. Walking down to the bus stop he saw a newspaper poster, bearing a heading in large black type. Two Women and One Man he read, and there were blurred photographs of the Wife, the Husband and the Other Woman, the latter's features obscured by a white patch. This served to remind him of the commonplace aspects of his situation. And he fell to recalling the various solutions men had reached in a similar predicament. Crippen had disposed of his wife for love of Ethel Le Neve. Thomas Wainwright, on the other hand, had shot his mistress and remained with his wife. Neither offered him any help, since both had been discovered and executed. The only man who could have aided him would have been one who had solved the problem and not been apprehended. Waiting for the bus he remembered the second letter in his pocket and opened this also. It was signed Mrs. M. Lockyer and was to the effect that Will had had a bad turn and had been rushed to hospital by ambulance. Mrs. Lockyer gave the name of the hospital, the number of the ward and the number of the bed. She didn't wish to importunate, she assured Henry (how well he knew that word on the lips of such as she and what dignity it conveyed), but Will kept asking for him and the doctor had warned her there wasn't much time. She had always known such a crisis might arrive without warning and so she had always been prepared. It would give Will so much pleasure if he, Henry, could look in just for a few minutes, and she was his respectfully . . . Henry thrust the letter into his pocket. Since Will was on the danger list the ordinary visiting hours, meticulously listed by the sick man's wife, wouldn't apply. He could receive a visitor at any time, and it was sheer folly for Henry to break his original plan and go direct to the hospital. First things first the brothers in London used to say, but surely Beverley and Beverley's future were more important than a sick man who might already be unconscious for all Henry knew. Yet, when he alighted from the bus, it was to the hospital that he turned his steps, against reason and inclination alike.

Will was very near the end. His wife was sitting with him, but she rose with a little gasp of pleasure as Henry came in.

" I'm sorry not to have come before," he said. " The fact is, I've been away "—the small lie rose easily to his lips—" and I only got your letter an hour ago."

" It was very good of you to come right away," said Mrs. Lockyer gratefully. " I only hope it wasn't very inconvenient."

He suppressed a wry smile at the thought of how very inconvenient it had been, and sat beside the dying man as though he had no other thought in the world. Mrs. Lockyer quietly withdrew. There was, after all, very little he could accomplish. For some minutes he wasn't even sure Will recognised his presence, but after a while he opened his eyes and, as though he were continuing a conversation broken off a couple of minutes earlier, he said, " For myself I don't hold with the Russik convention about the knights—you remember, sir? "

Henry wondered if he knew he was dying. He talked

quite sensibly for a time, then seemed to lose interest, and sank into the coma of indifference. Henry had the limp fingers in his, but when he tried to release himself Will stirred in distress.

Henry resumed his former position. " It's all right," he said, " I'm still here."

Presently Mrs. Lockyer came back. " It was good of you," she said humbly. " It was as if Will was just holding on till you came. It meant a lot to him, you coming every week the way you did. It was as if it was a link with life, and he hadn't many, my poor Will."

Henry knew what she meant, so did not commit the solecism of saying, " He had you." Will was the type that takes a wife for granted, not as a part of the outside world at all. Henry represented everything he could never hope for again, made him realise himself as still part of a living world. Henry never offered him sympathy or tried to find reasons for calamities or the idiosyncrasies of other men. People were as they were and life like a series of boxes all fitting inside each other. You could never be sure when you removed one what picture you would find on the one beneath.

The nurse came in presently and told Henry he could not do any good by waiting, and as Will's fingers insensibly relaxed Henry stood up and stretched some of the stiffness out of his bones. He promised to ring up later and find out if there was any news. He told Mrs. Lockyer that she knew where to get hold of him if she wanted anything he could supply, then he shook hands and went away.

" Who was that? " asked the nurse easily, bending above the sick man's bed.

" Mr. Browne," was Mrs. Lockyer's sedate reply. Not that she was deceived, though perhaps Will had been. A nom-de-plume as writers put it, some big pot, she wouldn't be surprised, not wanting to be identified, a Christian certainly by all reasonable standards, not wanting his right hand to know what his left hand did. Her heart swelled with generous gratitude for the little he had been able to do for her husband. Little? she would say. It was what Will wanted. A gold crown would not have meant a thing to Will, but these faithful visitations, with never a hint of patronage or boredom, well, she thought in a momentary burst of extravagance, I am sure men have been sainted for less.

It was all my eye, of course, but she really believed it.

Hurrying away, Henry almost collided with a dark stocky man who came rushing in as if the Income Tax collectors were after him.

" Sorry, sorry," said the man, a doctor called Potter, and as Henry vanished he said to the matron, who had appeared in the hall, " what's Henry Greatorex doing here? "

" Greatorex? "

" Yes. He nearly bowled me over as I came in."

" Oh, you must mean Mr. Browne. He's been visiting a case in Number 4."

" Oh, well," said Potter cheerfully, throwing off his overcoat, " they say we all have a double. How's the hysterectomy in 23? "

He forgot all about the brief encounter and never gave it another thought till he found the police on his doorstep, asking questions in connection with a murdered woman called Stella Foster.

CHAPTER V

LEAVING THE HOSPITAL on his way to Hallett Street Henry was aware of the strongest disinclination to proceed with his original plan. Crook would have called it a hunch and obeyed it; Henry, knowing his own weaknesses a deal better than most people realised, thought it was cowardice, because he dreaded what lay just ahead. A lazy man and peaceable, he detested the thought of violence, in spirit as in the flesh. And though he could be optimistic to the verge of folly, he could not believe that Stella would accept the compromise he had come to offer. And if she did not? A vision of Beverley rose before his eyes, Beverley whose life was threatened by this mad woman, Beverley, whom he must defend at all costs and at any risk.

The lights in the Fanshawes' house were all extinguished when he arrived. Joe was sitting at the back behind a drawn curtain, making the most of a brief period of untormented leisure, since Emily and her sister had gone to see Gregory Peck. A pencil of light gleamed between the curtains in Stella's sitting-room, which showed she was at home, waiting. A most unpleasant analogy occurred to him—the Spider and the Fly—the blonde implacable spider and the helpless fly. Helpless? His mind shrank away from the word and all its implications.

He was about to ring the bell when he noticed the door was on the latch, which made him suppose she was expecting a visitor whom she trusted. Stella had the townswoman's habit of keeping the doors locked and even bolted. If it was going to be a threesome the evening might have odd repercussions, and once again he thought of turning back and taking the bus to Beckfield. Having keyed himself up to the interview, however, he nerved himself to push the door open and stand listening for a moment. If she was anticipating another caller, that should shorten their interview; in his hopeless (and quite groundless) optimism he even thought it might aid his case, since she would hardly want X to arrive and find her embroiled in an argument in which the gun might, for the second time, be brought into play. There were voices coming from behind the closed door of the sitting-room and it was a moment before he realised it was only a radio programme running its course. Stella, like many solitary women, was a radio fiend; she kept the instrument running all day, whether she listened to the programmes or not. He dropped his hat and gloves on the chest, tossed away the cigarette he was smoking and opened the sitting-room door.

Stella was waiting for him, lying back on the settee.

As Henry swung the gate to behind him and marched up the path Mrs. Fanshawe and her sister turned the corner of the road.

" Did you see that? " hissed Emily. In moments of excitement she really did hiss. Joe said once it was like living in the Big Snake House at the Zoo. " Another one going in. Really, she might as well hang a red light over the door."

The sister said dryly that she might as well save the expense, since everyone seemed to know her address.

" I wonder if Joe noticed who it was," Mrs. Fanshawe continued, but, of course, Joe had not. It was in vain for him to protest that he was sitting on the other side of the house; Emily created the impression that a loyal husband would have taken the vacant place in the parlour window so as to be able to report to his wife on her return.

" Had a good time? " he added, quickly, hoping to soften her.

" A bit dry, I thought," she said, refusing to acknowledge pleasure even where it had been enjoyed.

He reflected, sighing, that nothing was ever quite right for her, not even her favourite movie star.

" Disgusting, I call it," his wife continued. " One of these days she'll be found with her throat cut and

serve her right, that's what I say. Come on, Lu, let's
put the kettle on and we'll take our tea into the front
room."

She struck a match and lighted the gas stove, produced
what she called a " gateau " from a tin box with a picture
of the young Queen on the lid and set the cups on the
tray. Joe waited till they had settled themselves and
oiled out of the back door down to the Coach and
Horses.

Even there he couldn't escape from the woman across
the road. A young fellow was asking the barmaid if
Mrs. Foster had come in that night. " Sent her a card
saying I'd be over," he explained.

The barmaid said indifferently she had not seen her,
maybe she was at the Horn of Plenty, but he said he had
been there first.

" You're out of luck, mate," said Joe. " She's at home
this evening. With a friend," he added. He had seen
the young chap once or twice before, he thought, and
they got into desultory conversation now. Any male
talk was a treat to him after the endless nattering of
Emily and her sister. He bought a pint and presently
joined in a darts game. For a blessed hour he could forget
that he was a married man.

In the house he had so thankfully left the two women
had settled themselves cosily by the parlour window.

" Half a sec. till I draw the curtain," Emily said.
" Oh! " Her voice drew Lu quickly to her side.

" What is it? "

" Must have noticed we were back," said Emily dryly.
" She's drawing her own curtains right across. If that
doesn't show a bad conscience I don't know what does.
Wonder what she's up to now."

But Stella, poor silly creature, was past being up to
anything. She had achieved all the mischief, all the fun,
all the success she was ever going to have. No man who
saw her now would desire her and all the mystery that
remained was: Who was responsible? and Why?

In Stella's sitting-room, shielded by the curtains he

had so cautiously closed, Henry stood staring, aghast, at the night's work. However he had intended it to end, it hadn't been like this. He couldn't really believe it even now, that she who had been first his love and then his companion and only his enemy during the past few weeks, should have come to this. He had been turning over the placatory phrases as he walked up to the house, had considered this argument and that, pushing away from him the appalling conclusion that had swept through his mind like a tearing wind on the night he had made his frantic journey to The Running Dog. If one must die, he had thought fiercely, it shall not be Beverley. But now that the dice were thrown and Stella had lost, he was trembling and shocked, couldn't pull himself together sufficiently to recognise his own peril, or even congratulate himself that there had been no watcher at the window to note his arrival. Death he had seen before, though not often; violent death he had never beheld, and now, finding himself in the centre of the calamity, knowing his own security hung by a hair, he was bewildered beyond the limits of common sense.

He had not anticipated that the crisis would blow up at such breakneck speed; the little gun lay on the carpet, and he stooped to lift it, then remembered that his fingerprints must not be found upon it and let it lie. However he had thought the interview would go it had not been like this. And how on earth had it happened? She should not, of course, have waved that little gun; it sent a man's blood into his brain, clouding his senses, so that the fatal action was taken before the will could be called into play. He had never understood till now that murder can be an instinctive act, without malice aforethought.

"Rats!" Crook would have said. "Murder begins in the mind. Whether you accept the fact or not, the will to murder is there before the deed's done. If you're so daft you don't know what's in your mind, that's too bad, but it won't frank you in the eyes of a jury."

He knew, too, the meaning of time standing still. He

could not think, his brain was paralysed. Only, some-where a warning bell rang, to remind him of that open door which showed that someone else was expected. He had heard men debating sometimes—how do murderers feel after a crime? Satisfied? Frightened? Cool-headed because an objective's been attained, no matter by what frightful means? He only knew that his predominating emotion was fear—not pity for Stella who, so short a time ago, had put on this new dress, set out the whisky bottle and glass and prepared for an hour of love, not even horror at this abrupt deflowering of her beauty, the shattering of her warmth and charm—only dread of what the future held and the consequences to himself. He compelled himself to cross the room and close the curtains, that was his only action to date. But now he realised that he must not be found here and began to consider what steps he should take for self-protection. What should he do first? Telephone the police, saying, " I came to visit Mrs. Foster and found her dead on arrival? " Was there any possibility of swinging *that*, in the face of circumstances that must become known when the inquiry started? Besides, to put himself in the centre of the picture must surely result in the loss of Beverley, even if he could persuade the police that his story was true. He was certain that Stella had never fathomed the truth of his identity; he had written her no letters, never taken her away for a surreptitious week-end, had paid her allowance in notes of small denominations. If he could retreat unperceived, wasn't there a chance that his name would never be connected with her death?

He found that he was muttering to himself. " I never dreamed that it would be like this," he said, and in a momentary flash of grim humour wondered how many other men fighting for their lives had said the same. His heart beat so loud he half expected to hear the swing of the gate as neighbours came up to know what was amiss. His own staff would not have recognised the cool, bland Henry Greatorex they had known for twenty years.

This, he thought, is why criminals, having planned an act down to the last detail, suddenly lose heart, give themselves up, let everything for which they've struggled float away from them.

The struggle had been very short; Stella had not anticipated the attack, though in the brief moments remaining to her she had fought for her life. A dented cushion lay on the floor, the cover of the settee was wrinkled, a little vase of flowers had been overturned and the water made a dark patch on the pale carpet. He thrust his hands into his pockets, because he had read somewhere that every material retained fingerprints. He drew out a handkerchief and wiped the handle of the door, considered flinging the drawers wide and scattering the contents to give the impression of murder for gain, but here his legal experience came to his aid. Give the police as little help as possible. He stood staring about him, wondering if he could be identified by the presents he had given her over the years, nothing of striking value, a brooch, a handbag, a silk umbrella, a necklace of coloured stones. . . . A newspaper lay on a side table and he read the headline numbly. TRAINS COLLIDE it said. Seventeen dead in wreckage. It didn't appear to make any sense. Seventeen people killed in a train accident—it would probably be nineteen or twenty by to-morrow—and one woman killed in her own home. She would be headlines in the morning, attracting as much attention as, perhaps more than, the anonymous seventeen.

The sound of feet going past in the street awakened him to a sense of urgency. He stepped back from the room, leaving the radio playing and the light ablaze. It wouldn't be safe to risk departure by the front door, not with that female vulture at the window opposite. He recalled how often Stella had complained about Mrs. Fanshawe. I hardly feel safe in my bath, she had said. Fortunately, the house had a back entry, though it was seldom used, only, he thought, by the dust collector who brought his cart down the narrow lane leading from the High Street. Tiptoeing, as though an incautious step might wake her, he collected his hat and gloves and made his way to the rear of the house. The key turned quietly into the lock, and he was out in the drizzling dark. In summer weather the lane was a well-known rendezvous for lovers, since it was a cul-de-sac, and most of the Hallett Street tenants, like Stella, never used their back entry, but on such an evening there was no one abroad. He hungered for a cigarette to soothe his nerves, but dared not kindle even a momentary flame, lest someone should be peering from an upper window. He found the numbness that had originally assailed his mind had now transferred itself to his flesh, and he stood for some minutes in the kindly dark, until he had regained control of his limbs. There was not a light to be seen anywhere in the little lane, and for that he thanked his stars; he thanked, too, the actual stars in the heavens above him that were obscured by the misty rain. So, at last, hurrying, clinging to the wall, he made his way back to the High Street.

A cheerfully lighted snack bar stood on the corner and he wished he dared go in and buy himself some coffee, but instinct warned him to get free of Martindale as soon as he could. There were only a few people about, and he pulled his hat over his eyes as he emerged into the lights. A man coming in the opposite direction almost ran against him, but he swerved and avoided the contact. A little farther along the pavement he saw a policeman and for the first time in his life he flinched before the presence of the law. The policeman was engaged in re-fastening a waterproof cape and later, when questions were asked, had to confess, with chagrin, that he had noticed no one. It would have been a feather in a young constable's cap if he had been able to give evidence about an escaping criminal.

Mrs. Fanshawe, immovable at her window as an exhibit at Madame Tussaud's, saw a man walk up the street and push open the gate of No. 17.

" Wait for it! " she warned Lu. " Madam's got her

tricks mixed for once. That first fellow hasn't come out yet. What's going to happen when the second one finds he's been double-crossed?"

All that happened, of course, was that the second visitor got no reply to his pealing of the bell and, when that proved ineffective, his tapping on the coloured glass panels of the front door. He stood back staring at the parlour window where it was still possible to discern a gleam of light. He made another attempt, even peeping through the letter box, but it did him no good. No one came out, and after another minute or so he shrugged his shoulders and went away. Afterwards it was demonstrated that he could not have missed Henry by more than a minute or so, must indeed have met him face to face if Henry had left the house by the front door.

Henry did not pause until he had reached a public house called the Clarendon Arms, where he might hope to catch a bus back to Beckfield, but, finding he had still nearly half an hour to wait, he walked on. At the corner of Brattle Street and Abbey Green he saw a coffee stall set up for the benefit of night travellers, and stopped to buy coffee and a meat pie. His appearance here attracted no attention, since there was a local cinema close at hand whose devotees were the chief clients at this hour. Half a mile beyond this was another bus stop and here the omnibus caught up with him and whirled him back to Beckfield. Thanks to the inclement night the passengers were mostly muffled and silent, and he had little fear of being recognised. It was almost ten o'clock when he alighted near the Castle Hotel at Beckfield and went into the saloon bar. Passing through the room he noticed Avery sitting alone at a small table, the inevitable Mr. Smith in attendance.

Henry paused. "I shall be looking to you for that occasional game of chess," he warned his nephew. "I've just been saying good-bye to my old friend and faithful opponent." In a few more words he told Avery of Will Lockyer's sudden attack and imminent death. "I left the widow at the hospital," he added, " but it's doubtful if he recovers consciousness. It was a matter of hours when I left a short time ago." He frowned. " I hope someone will see her back to Burns Row, if she doesn't spend the night at the hospital," he added.

He was moving away when Avery, changed from his nephew and understudy to the sharp-eyed invigilator, inquired, " Has Mrs. Lockyer any children? "

Henry stared in amazement. " My dear fellow! How on earth should I know? I've never heard either of them speak of any, and I should think it improbable."

" But she has relations, I suppose? "

" Oh, I should think so," Henry agreed. " Very few people are immune."

Avery now reflected his uncle's astonishment. " Don't you really know ? "

" My dear fellow, why should I? I'm not a social welfare officer. I went there once a week to play chess with Will, and Martha Lockyer used to bring us a glass of beer afterwards. That's practically all I know about them."

" After five years? " Avery still looked dumbfounded.

" How much more would you have known? "

" Roughly everything," was Avery's spirited reply.

" How on earth would you have found out? "

" They'd have told me."

" Only if you'd questioned them, and who the devil was I to ask them about their private affairs? They never catechised me about mine."

" What's the widow going to live on? " continued Avery in vigorous tones.

" My dear Avery, I haven't the smallest idea. I suppose she'll have a pension."

" Does she go out to work? "

" I begin to think," commented Henry, grimly, " it's a good thing I didn't implement my suggestion of your giving Will a game. I should probably have found the catch up next time I called at Burns Row. My dear boy, have you never heard of ordinary give-and-take? So far as I can gather, with you it's cut-and-thrust. If Martha Lockyer wants any help, there are half a dozen organisations to whom she can apply."

"You were on the spot," Avery pointed out.

"As a friend. People don't want their friends nosing into their personal lives. If ever I'm down and out I shall make for the aseptic atmosphere of the National Assistance Board. I have rights there. That's the gospel of our day."

He laughed shortly at Avery's perplexed face and moved on, feeling unaccountably ruffled. He was also startled to realise that for two or three minutes he had actually forgotten about Stella Foster. From his solitary table across the room he saw the young man wearing a look too old for his years. That boy has seen too much, he reflected. He must have gone into the army practically from school, and turned to his philanthropic labours as soon as he was out of uniform. Why doesn't he get a girl or go on a bender or do any of the things normal fellows do at his age? If he goes on like this he'll end in a monastery, where," he decided with characteristic humour, "he'll be considerably less of a reproach to ordinary selfish chaps like me."

But he did not brood about Avery for long. The ghost of Stella returned to torment him; and he was teased, moreover, by a nagging conviction that he had overlooked something of importance, something he could not identify, some person or fact who would eventually bring down his house of cards. He puzzled over this conviction all the evening, but when at last, in the small hours, he took himself to bed, the problem remained unsolved.

In another household not ten miles distant Stella Foster was also under discussion that evening. Muriel Sumner was fiddling with the TV set, waiting for the weather forecast, when the front-door bell rang and she heard Mrs. Hogg cross the hall to answer it. The voice of her sister, Dorothy Hunter, came clearly to her ears.

"'Evening, Mrs. Hogg." Dorothy dropped her coat in the hall and plunged into the sitting-room. "Oh, Mu, turn that off. I don't see why you bother to have a set when not one vehicle in a hundred is fitted with a suppressor. I suppose someone's running a Hoover or an electric razor," she added, watching the lines of electrical disturbance chase across the screen.

Her sister switched off. " It's Gerry," she explained. " He likes it. I never wanted a set."

" Oh, yes, Gerry." Dorothy flung herself into Gerald's favourite chair. " I've got a bone to pick with him. Next time you marry, Mu, don't take something out of the Large Rat House. The Zoo," she added explanatorily, as her sister's eyes rested wonderingly on her face.

Muriel stooped to pick up a magazine. " What on earth were you doing in the Zoo? " she asked, absently.

" Oh, Mu, don't you ever listen? Of course I haven't been near the Zoo. I only said next time you marry . . ."

A sound made her turn her head. Scotch Mrs. Hogg had come in and was standing there, a look of frozen disapproval on her face. Dorothy knew that she scorned everything about her, her make-up, her long fingernails, her racy clothes and, above all, her spinster estate.

" Will the master be in to dinner, Mrs. Sumner? " she inquired, frostily.

" Didn't I tell you? " Muriel looked startled. " He telephoned, he's been kept in London—an unexpected appointment."

" Oh, rats! " ejaculated Dorothy. " He's no more in London than I am. He was on my train. I must say," she added, thoughtfully, " he made every effort not to be noticed. I bawled after him for a lift, but he rushed away as if I were Faust and he Marguerite."

" What nonsense you talk! " Muriel spoke sharply. " He's in London. You saw someone who looked like him . . ."

" Also with a grey Bentley. What a coincidence, as that comic on the wireless says."

" Quite a coincidence," agreed her sister, so quietly that Dorothy took fright. She saw the woman still standing on the threshold, her hands hanging limply at her sides. " I do wish you'd think before you speak," scolded Muriel as soon as the door had closed behind Mrs. Hogg. " Even if you do think you saw Gerry you could have played up, couldn't you? Luckily, she's no gossip, but she's the world's puritan, and she'll read the most lascivious scandal into your remarks. If you knew what it's like trying to get a cook in the country you'd be more careful. Only let her get an idea that Gerry's leading a loose life . . ."

" Why, Mu! " For there were tears in her sister's eyes. " I'm sorry, old girl, really I am. Honestly, I did see him. How was I to know he was travelling incog.? Of course, he never telephoned . . ."

" He did telephone. Gerry always does the right thing. He had an appointment."

" I don't doubt it. But not in London. I thought it was rum. The road from the station here is pretty long and straight, only one deviation in the Crosfield-Martindale direction, but I never caught sight of Gerry in my taxi. So that's his little game." She whistled softly. " And then you take me to task about not being married."

" I don't care if you marry a blackamoor or live in sin with a Turk," exclaimed Muriel in exasperated tones. " All I beg of you is don't ruin my marriage. By that I mean don't fall on Gerry as soon as he comes in and ask him why he didn't stop and give you a lift. It won't help me in the least, in fact it'll probably start a persecution mania with Gerry. You know how he hates interference, even more than most men. I daren't even tidy his desk."

" You mean, you knew he was up to a little game," exclaimed Dorothy, crudely. " Honestly, Mu, I think you're round the bend. If I had a husband . . ."

" He'd probably beat you black and blue and he'd have my sympathy," interrupted Muriel. " Can you get it into your head that I'm in love with my husband, and don't intend to part with him to Circe and the Witch of Endor rolled into one? Oh, yes." She put up a nervous hand and pushed some hair off her forehead. " I never believed in the sudden business appointment. It's no use trying to explain to you, Dot, you don't know Gerry. He's the world's romantic, what we used to call an idealist. Every so often he discovers the world's perfect woman and he's after her like a greyhound after an electric hare. Oh, it doesn't last, he always finds he's been misled, and in any case it's something to remember that once I was his ideal woman, and I'm still the only one he married. Did you never guess he was like that? " she added.

" I knew he was impressionable, of course. I haven't forgotten that night at the Nell Gwynn. He couldn't take his eyes off this woman." She stopped, drawing a sharp breath. " Mu, that isn't the one? "

" Oh, I expect so. I recognised the symptoms that night, but get this into your head, Dot, there's nothing to be done about it. Oh, I could make a scene, threaten divorce, and what would happen? Gerry would say, All right, go ahead, and I shouldn't be able to draw back, and at the end of six months or so I'd be worse off than you, for at least you've got a job, and I shouldn't have anything."

" I couldn't see what he saw in her, could you? " asked Dorothy, innocently. " She wasn't even pretty, she wasn't young, a pasty-faced creature, all angles—and she looked about as animated as a doll."

" Anyone could tell you weren't married, Dot." There was nothing unkind in the voice. " It's no use believing that men and women use the same yardstick when it comes to assessing values. Think of the number of times you've heard men say, I can't imagine what she sees in that chap. Well? "

" Well—yes," Dorothy acknowledged.

" And haven't you sometimes wanted to tell them? Because it was perfectly obvious to you. I agree, she wasn't very young, she was as white as a sheet and she hadn't bothered much about make-up; in fact, she looked half-witted—but that didn't prevent practically every man in the room staring at her as if she were Robinson

Crusoe's footprint. Even that man who looked like an orang-utan in a chocolate suiting wasn't proof against her. And that sort of woman isn't in that state because she's lost her purse or someone's been unkind to her. There was a man behind that—and she was feeling as I'd feel if I knew I'd lost Gerry for good—desperate, sick with her own pain."

" I've never heard you so eloquent," said Dorothy, frankly. " Do you really mean you're going to sit by and do nothing? Oh, I know about him being your husband and all that, but now you know the sort of man he is . . ."

" He's no different from the man I married. I just know him better, that's all. If there's a change in either of us, it's in me. I love him even more now than I did twenty years ago. It's all I can do not to let him see it, and, of course, that would be fatal—like blackmail, at a time like this. Of course, I hate it, of course I'd like to scratch her eyes out, but we'd none of us be any better off, and quite soon Gerry will find he's been led up the garden again. No one could be as wonderful as he expects a woman to be. There's one consolation, he's getting older, and he can't keep up this sort of thing for ever. I'm pinning my hopes on a Darby and Joan set-up when we are both about seventy. It wouldn't surprise me if we qualified for the Dunmow Flitch as the most amiable couple of the year."

" And you're prepared to put up with an unfaithful husband for another fifteen years? "

" It's only intermittent, and this affair won't last long. I shall know when it's drawing to a close. Oh, not because he'll tell me, but he'll buy the woman of the moment some fantastically handsome present and that'll mean the end's in sight."

" It may be months," objected Dorothy, but Muriel shook her head.

" No. He's bought the present, a diamond wrist-watch from Perry's. Oh, it's the old story the novelists daren't use any more because it's such an old hat, but it's still true. The jeweller's bill in the pocket of the suit to go to the cleaners; I found it yesterday."

" Perry's of Bond Street," mused Dorothy. " Gerry flies high, doesn't he? "

" Only the best for Gerry. I get what consolation I can out of the thought that I was once the best, and at least I'm the only one he'll ever marry while there's breath in my body."

" I wonder you don't murder her," said Dorothy, simply.

" So that Gerry can go through life believing he once found the perfect woman and I robbed him of her? No, no, you have to let Gerry make his own discoveries. But all the same," she added with sudden violence, " nothing would please me more than to hear that someone else had."

Gerald Sumner came in shortly after nine o'clock and went straight to the television set which he turned on. There was a boxing programme advertised for this evening, and as a younger man he had been handy with the gloves. He did not seem disposed to talk, and though Dorothy asked him spitefully how the appointment in London had gone he refused to be drawn. Muriel tired early and said she would go to bed. Gerald raised no objection, he said he had some letters to write before he came up. But he made no move to write them, stayed in his chair staring at the television screen.

The next programme was professional magic. " Mu looks fagged," said Gerald, absently. " I suppose she's been rushing about all day. I wonder how these chaps do it," he went on, nodding towards the screen.

Anger boiled up in Dorothy's loyal heart. " You should know," she retorted. " Gerald Sumner, the man who can be in two places at once."

He turned quickly. " Joke? "

" Not to Muriel. If you must lie to her you might make certain of your facts first. I told you I was going to London to-day."

" What's this in aid of, Dot? Ought I to have taken you out to lunch or something? Actually, you didn't tell me . . ."

" You don't listen. You're like all men," retorted his sister-in-law in her sweeping fashion. " But it's a mistake. You see, I saw you get off my train at Pheasant Green at 7.10."

" Nonsense," returned Gerald. " I was in London. I had to deal with a specification for a Youth Hostel in the north." Gerald was partner in a well-known firm of architects. " In fact, I had dinner on the train."

" In another minute," gibed Dot, " you'll be telling me what you had to eat."

" What does the service ever offer you but stewed steak or minced chicken? Did you repeat this idiotic story to Muriel? "

" Of course. I told her I'd seen you and given you a hail, but you were off like a bat out of hell."

Gerald picked up an evening paper that he had brought in. He held it out a little way off.

" Pretty girl, don't you think? " he suggested, casually, indicating a photograph.

" I can't see at that distance," said Dot dryly.

" Really? But you could recognise me the whole length of the platform. Come off it, my dear girl. I wasn't there. If I had been I'd have come home to dinner." He began to feel in his pockets. " I may even have kept the bill," he murmured. " You know how it is, you shove 'em in your pocket . . ."

" I'd no idea you were so methodical. Could it be you expected to be questioned? "

" Not at all. But I keep accounts, and so I hold on to my receipts until the end of the day. I haven't done the accounts yet."

" I can see you're very practised." Gerald was still rummaging in his pockets and now he triumphantly held up a slip of paper. " There, does that convince you? "

" I prefer the evidence of my own eyes," said Dot, coolly.

" Having just demonstrated how unreliable they are. Look here, have you been talking like this to Muriel? "

" I told her I'd seen you. Not that she was surprised. She knew all about this beastly intrigue of yours. You're not very subtle, Gerry. I should think the whole of the Nell Gwynn could see, even before you pretended you'd lost your scarf and had to go back for it. You went back for her, didn't you? "

" I went back for my scarf," said Gerald, steadily. " And I met a chap I knew and we stayed on having a couple. You should be careful, Dorothy. You'll get yourself into serious trouble one of these days."

" Look who's talking," jeered Dorothy, beside herself with rage. " How about the watch? "

" The . . . ? "

" Muriel knows about that, too. A diamond-studded watch from Perry's. Sometimes, Gerald, you keep too many bits of paper and forget where you've left them."

" Do I understand you've been snooping among my things? " His voice was quiet now, which should have warned her. He was a man of hearty temper, quite capable of throwing things about or even setting the house on fire, if driven to it. It didn't mean much, he would have told you, just self-expression. It was when he kept calm that it was wise to watch your step.

" Not me. I don't send your suits to the cleaners."

" I see. So Muriel knows about that? A pity. I meant it to be a surprise."

" It was a surprise all right," Dorothy assured him.

" I don't mean that kind. But it's our anniversary next month and Muriel's been complaining about her watch not keeping good time, so I thought . . ." He put his hand in his pocket. " Since the secret's out you may as well give me your opinion. Do you think she'll like it? " He slipped the lid off the little box with Perry's name scrawled across it in gold lettering, to reveal the charming little gaud nestling in its bed of cotton wool.

" Oh, I never doubted you could pick them," agreed Dorothy, bitterly. " Yes, it's a little pet, but I don't think my sister is going to appreciate being offered your mistress's leavings. Of course, it was meant for that woman, you don't pull the wool over my eyes so easily. If you'd really meant it for Muriel, why are you carrying it about with you? "

" Perhaps because I feel it would be safer in my pocket than lying loose in a household with a professional snooper in it."

" If you hadn't something to hide you wouldn't worry about snoopers," Dorothy assured him, brazenly. " I suppose the truth is she's turned you down—or you found you'd been forestalled—so you had to bring it back. And as a good businessman you don't want to waste it. But I warn you, Gerry, if you don't make an end with that woman and give Mu a square deal you'll be sorry you were ever born."

She marched out of the room, slamming the door firmly behind her. Gerald lay back in his chair as though the scene had exhausted him to the point of collapse. Presently he picked up the little watch and stared at it. Before he went upstairs he drew his pen from his pocket and wrote on a card he took from a drawer: In Memory of Twenty Happy Years.

Then he tied up the little box and, still wearing that air of strain, carried it upstairs.

CHAPTER VI

EMILY FANSHAWE remained glued to the window pane till eleven o'clock that evening, in spite of her husband's repeated requests to give over and come to bed.

"If he hasn't gone yet you take my word, he's spending the night there," he warned her. "And it's his business anyway, not yours."

"That's just like you," retorted his wife. "It's not my business how immoral people are, I suppose."

"Didn't know they'd made you a member of the Watch Committee," agreed Joe Fanshawe. "It's my belief you're jealous of her."

That brought her flaming back into the room, as he had known it would. "Jealous? Of a creature like that?"

"She's got what it takes," suggested Joe Fanshawe. "Ever noticed her eyes? I've told you, you should come to the Coach and Horses sometimes."

"So that's where she finds her fancy men? I might have guessed. P'raps that's why you're so keen on going out of an evening. You be careful, Joe Fanshawe. You never did have much sense. Not that you'd be worth anything to a bad lot like that."

"Well, since we've decided that point, how about a bit of shut-eye?" suggested Joe, pacifically.

"You go up, if you like. I've one or two things to do."

"Why don't you go over and ring the bell? P'raps he has cut her throat. That 'ud be a thrill for you. Or p'raps she's turned on the gas." He yawned and rose. "Don't forget I got to go to work in the morning, Em. I don't want you crawling in beside me as cold as a stone about one a.m."

Emily turned furiously to her sister. "When you lost Truman perhaps it wasn't such a bit of bad luck as you thought at the time," she said fiercely. "Talk about cutting throats. There's times I hardly trust myself with the carving-knife."

"Oh, go on, Em," said her sister, affectionately. "Joe's all right. A sight better than George ever was. Anyway, you don't have to go out cleaning to pay the rent. Lucky for me he was killed in an accident and not falling over his own feet coming back from the Blue Boar. First time I'd seen any real money for years."

Half an hour later she also yawned prodigiously and asked, "Isn't there a back way out of those houses same as ours? Well, then, that's probably where he went. If not, Joe's right, and you'll be here till morning."

Emily looked ill with disappointment. "I never thought. You could be right, Lu. Well, that proves something. He's always come out as clear as daylight before. It wouldn't surprise me if we were all to find ourselves in the papers before the end of the week."

Even Arthur Crook couldn't have produced a better hunch.

The next morning Emily was busy with her usual duties, went out, shopped, stopped for a nice cup of tea at the Flopsy Bunny Café, and got back about midday. Joe, thank goodness, got his lunch (only he called it dinner, not being the kind that knows how to raise himself, she told Lu) at the works canteen, so she didn't have to bother about that. She brought in a paper of fried fish and chips for herself and Lu. It was when they were sitting over another pot of tea (in the parlour, of course, since the kitchen was at the back of the house with no outlook whatever for an enterprising woman who took an interest in her neighbours), that something struck Lu as being odd.

"Notice anything funny, Em?"

Emily did not have to inquire what she meant, she knew it was something about the house opposite that had caught her sister's attention. She went over to the window.

"She hasn't drawn the sitting-room curtains," she

announced. " Having a late morning, sleeping it off, I suppose."

" Think so? " said Lu in significant tones, lifting her eyes to the floor above.

" Good grief, she never pulled the bedroom curtains last night. That is—they're open now, and if they're open then why are the others still shut? "

" There's more than that," said Lu. " She's never taken her milk off the step—or her bread. It's never there this time of day. Her ladyship's ever so particular."

" You're right, Lu. There is something up. She never has bread two days running, and she had a loaf yesterday, I saw the man leave it."

" Unless she's having a party," suggested Lu doubtfully.

" On a half pint of milk? Be your age, Lu. No, I'll tell you what it is, she's never come down this morning to change the markers."

Stella was what Emily would have described as a one for gadgets; she had a little wooden toy featuring a coy female and a black cat with a moveable tail. The female's arm could be used as an indicator for the milkman's benefit—half a pint, a pint, a quart and so forth. Similarly the cat's tail showed how much bread was required.

" And that's the way it was yesterday morning," insisted Emily. The Recording Angel had little on her when it came to knowing facts about her neighbours. " It's what's called a bow at a venture, what Joe said last night, I mean. You take my word for it, she hasn't come down this morning because she can't."

" Blind? " asked Lu innocently.

" Stiff," was Emily's grim retort. " The next time she comes out of that house, Lu, it'll be in a box." She brooded. " Lu, I'm going to the police."

Lu, who lived in London where you are not encouraged to poke your nose into your neighbours' affairs, looked startled.

" What are you going to tell them? That she hasn't come down to take in the milk? There's no law makes you do that."

" I'll go over and ring the bell," decided Emily.
" Suppose she opens the door? "
" I'll just say I was afraid she was ill and is there any-
thing we can do, being neighbours like."

She put on a hat, she even carried gloves, and sailed
across the road. But she met with no better fortune than
the latest of Stella's overnight visitors. No one came
down, no one looked out of the window, no one stirred
on the other side of the door. Only, faint and dreamy,
the sound of the radio playing on and on, came to their
ears as they waited on the step.

" Well, that proves one thing," said Emily, energetically.
" That young chap didn't get in last night because there
wasn't anyone at home who could open the door; and
the other chap didn't come out by the front because he
didn't dare show his face."

It was Lu, her imagination jumping ahead, who
suggested that there might be two corpses behind the
closed door, but Emily retorted disdainfully that though
men were fools they couldn't be silly enough to go throwing away their lives for a strumpet like that. And then,
grasping Lu firmly by the arm, she guided her firmly
down to the police station.

When Henry opened his paper the same morning he
found no mention of Stella's name, which seemed to prove
that so far she had not been found. He supposed vaguely
that the longer interval that elapsed before discovery
the better for a murderer. It was unfortunate in a way
that Greatorex Brothers never handled crimes of violence,
it gave him no experience on which to rely. All through
the day Henry appeared his normal self. Only Addie
Bainbridge, with her sixth sense where he was concerned,
was convinced something was amiss. He telephoned the
hospital and learned that Will had died in the small hours
of the morning without recovering consciousness, and
arranged with a Martindale florist to send a wreath to
the Burns Row house. He would not attend the funeral,
he thought, knowing that Mrs. Lockyer would take no

offence at his absence. From this day on he must move with circumspection, think twice before he spoke, keep watch over his lightest word. This caution was new to him and reinforced his understanding of guilty men throwing up the sponge and abandoning themselves to the law, driven by the prickly goad of unbearable suspense.

The evening papers from London reached Beckfield about five o'clock; once again there was no news of Stella. But the local paper appeared on Thursdays, and " That'll be the day," reflected Henry grimly, " that'll be the day."

And at about the same time as he reached this conclusion the police had started their search for the murderer of Stella Foster.

Not that they had displayed any enthusiasm when the dauntless Mrs. Fanshawe, her more reluctant sister in tow, marched into the station. They had nothing to go on, said the local officer.

" You don't know her," insisted Emily. " She'd never leave her milk out there all day. Be afraid a dicky-bird would come down and have a peck. To say nothing of the bread."

She dragged the protesting constable round to Hallett Street. Miss Mence, with Sandy in tow, was standing at the gate.

" Seen anything of her ladyship to-day? " demanded Emily.

" Her husband's just died." Miss Mence spoke as though she had personally attended the death-bed.

" Husband? " snorted Emily, and the little old maid repeated, " Yes, her husband. And she's going to marry again. She told me the day she asked me about the letter."

" Letter? " exclaimed the police constable. Lu gave her sister a nudge. " What letter's that? "

" I don't really know, she didn't show it to me, but she seemed very upset. Talked about people being had up for writing letters or something."

" That shows we're not the only ones to object to her carryings-on," put in Emily, brazenly. Lu stared. " Why did she come to you? " her sister went on. " Had you written it? "

" Of course not. I didn't even know her, and, as I said, if I had anything to say I wouldn't need to put it in a letter, not with her living next door."

The policeman tried to sort out the story; he was beginning to think there might be something in Emily's suspicion. Like last night's visitor, like Emily and Lu, he got no response.

" Why don't you try the back ? " Emily suggested, and Miss Mence invited them all to use her house as a passage-way. It would save them quite a tramp, she said, almost coquettishly.

The back door of Stella's house proved unlocked, and the three women crowded in behind P.C. Brett. No one challenged them and though he paused to call, " Mrs. Foster? Are you at home? " no one answered.

Stella had not moved since Henry left the house the previous night, and even to an officer whose sole experience of violent death had been a motor-cycle collision, it was clear she would never move again. Lu, looking over Emily's shoulder, let out a shriek that made Sandy jump out of his mistress's arms and bite the police officer in the leg. Miss Mence snatched him up.

" I'll take him home," she gulped. " It's not a fit sight for anyone sensitive."

Even the doughty Emily was looking pale. Lu was beyond speech. P.C. Brett said in a queer voice, " Do either of you ladies know where the telephone 'ud be? " But there was no telephone installed, so he closed the house, shoo-ing the not reluctant women before him, and went down to report to the sergeant, grateful for once that he had not yet earned his stripes.

Inspector Wilfred Davis was put in charge of the murder, and proceeded, with the aid of the usual squad of back-room boys, to build up a case. The house itself yielded two clues, a postcard that had arrived on the Wednesday morning, reading: " Passing through to-

morrow, hope to see you. Happy landings. P.," and
a cigarette stub that had been pitched down in the hall.
The postcard was the kind to be seen on seaside kiosks
and in the windows of small sweet shops, highly coloured,
audaciously designed and piquantly captioned. The
cigarette stub bore no maker's name and was hand-made
and of fine quality.

It was the postcard that caught the public interest.
The enterprising *Gazette* published a reproduction of the
addressed side, with the heading:

MURDERED WOMAN'S MYSTERY CORRESPONDENT
WHO IS " P "?

But Davis paid more attention to the cigarette. " Made
for some fussy customer," he announced. " It's barely
possible that he and ' P ' are identical, but I should doubt
it. This kind of tobacco doesn't go with comic-landlady
stuff." He turned back to the stub. " Should yield us a
fingerprint; it was thrown away, not stubbed out, which
looks as though the chap who smoked it was pretty well
at home in the house. Can't have been the dead woman's,
since it's established that she didn't smoke. No proof yet,
but it wouldn't surprise me to know that the chap who
smokes these is also responsible for the rent." For he had
wasted no time in learning something of the dead woman's
history. This was less easy than it sounded, since it was
difficult to obtain unprejudiced information. The general
view was that Mrs. Foster was stand-offish, didn't make
friends easily among the locals, though she had no trouble
in finding escorts and companions in the two bars she
frequented. She dressed stylishly, according to Martindale
standards, and did not appear to be short of money. She
still carried on her dressmaking business, but more, it was
believed, for the casual contacts it brought her, than
because the money was important. She had had a
regular Friday visitor for some years, and other visitors,
invariably of the male sex, on other evenings. No one had
any information as to the identity of Friday's child, as

Davis called him, but Mrs. Fanshawe rushed in to say that on a number of occasions recently a grey Bentley car had either called at the door or been left in the car park while the owner came up to Hallett Street on foot.

"The way she tells it you'd think it meant climbing a mountain," observed Davis. "The car park's only about a hundred yards distant."

It was hardly to be expected that the owner of the Bentley should venture into the limelight. Nor did he. And Henry Greatorex also emulated Brer Rabbit, in that he lay low and said nuffin.

The patient investigations of the police produced a Mrs. Shrubsole, the tenant of No. 10, who said she had seen a man going down the lane behind Hallett Street on the night of Stella Foster's death. She fixed the time at nine o'clock, with a perfectly reasonable explanation for her assurance.

"Big Ben had just started striking on the news," she said, "when kitty suddenly began to mew loudly outside the window. Mr. Shrubsole says kitty must have had political affiliations before she came to us—his joke, see? —because she always come in when we put on the nine o'clock news. No, I didn't notice him particularly, in fact, he was just a hat and a dark shape going past the bottom of the garden, but I did pass the remark to Mr. Shrubsole, 'There's an optimist for you, if he thinks any girl's going to be waiting for him in this weather,' because it was drizzling again, nasty spiteful drizzle. Mr. Shrubsole said, 'Perhaps he's going to meet her at the back gate,' but not as if he was interested, which he wasn't. I tell him he and kitty are two of a kind—just sitting round that wireless at nine o'clock as if they could change the world if they gave their minds to it."

She had nothing more to add; she had not seen X again, either alone or in company, but then she had not opened the curtains after letting kitty in, and what with the voice of the man reading the news and the tap running when she went to fill the kettle for the cuppa they always had afterwards, well, you would not really expect it, would you? she inquired reasonably.

Equally reasonable, Davis agreed that he wouldn't. Mrs. Shrubsole's story explained why Mrs. Fanshawe had failed to see the 8.30 visitor leave No. 17. He was someone who knew his way about the house, and had very sensibly chosen to get out by the back entry.

" It was bad luck for him that Mrs. S.'s cat should be so precocious," added Davis. " X couldn't guess she was suddenly going to open the window and release a flood of light on to the lane. It's no wonder he put his head down and beat it as fast as he could."

He did not agree with Mrs. Shrubsole that the chap might have been keeping a rendezvous, and of course he was right.

It appeared to follow, therefore, that the murderer had arrived at eight-thirty and left the house a minute or so before nine. And what was he doing in the house for half an hour if he wasn't throttling Mrs. Foster?

He made further inquires at the Horn of Plenty where Bob Tanner behind the bar said, No, he couldn't tell the inspector much about the dead woman, she came in quite often, mostly alone, but generally left in company. He could not name any particular person she seemed to favour, it was just that she was jolly and friendly and men liked her. He didn't know (*stiffly*) if her escorts only took her as far as her gate or went into the house and had one for the road. He said in a very dry voice that it was not his affair.

" Murder's every citizen's affair," Davis, equally dry, reminded him. " Did she come in that night? "

" Matter of fact, she didn't. I remember there was a chap asking for her—and I haven't got his name and address either, he wasn't one of the regulars. He left a message for her—tell her Pete's been in, going on to the Coach and Horses, he said. Dunno if he found her there, she never came along to the Horn that night."

" You'd all have had screaming fits if she had," Davis told him, more dryly than ever. He was remembering the postcard. *Passing through to-morrow, hope to see you. Happy landings. P.* Funny, if the chap hadn't something on his conscience, that he hadn't come forward. Unless, of course, he was another candidate for the Crematorium Stakes.

"Remember what time this was?" he asked Bob.

Bob frowned. "Wouldn't like to be too sure," he admitted. "Say eight to eight-thirty, I wouldn't put it closer than that."

"Eight-thirty," said Davis in thoughtful tones. At eight-thirty Mrs. Fanshawe and Lu had seen a man going into Mrs. Foster's house. It was beginning to add up.

But it wasn't so simple, because when he went on to the Coach and Horses the girl behind the bar also remembered a tall, fair young fellow asking for Mrs. Foster. She wouldn't put a definite time to it, but remembered that he'd been talking to one of the regulars, Joe Fanshawe, who lived just opposite No. 17. She could add little about the young man; he had been in before and from something she had overheard she thought he was married, but of course, she added, he might just be shooting a line.

"Shooting a line?" repeated Davis, puzzled.

"In case any of the girls got ideas," explained the girl. "Not that he was any temptation to me. I've got my lines, had them these five years, and not wanting any change, thank you."

Joe Fanshawe said he had cleared out for a bit of peace and quiet after his wife and her sister got in from the pictures. They had just seen some chap go into No. 17, so if that was eight-thirty he had been round at the Coach and Horses eight-forty, say. The young chap had been there when he arrived. Yes, he had asked about Mrs. Foster and he (the witness) had said she wasn't likely to be coming along, she had got a friend visiting. They had talked for a little but he could not recall anything particular they said, and pretty soon he had got into a darts game.

So that, reflected Davis, appeared to let " P " out. He couldn't be the eight-thirty visitor, since Mrs. Fanshawe would have seen him leave, and it was established that he was in the Coach and Horses by eight-forty. He might be the mysterious man who called at nine o'clock, of course.

" Since Mrs. Fanshawe can testify that he didn't get in you'd expect him to show up, wouldn't you? " suggested P.C. Oliver, guilelessly.

Davis smiled. " That just shows your inexperience," he said. "Not a married man, I take it? No. But one of these days most likely you will be—probably won't have much say in the matter—and when you are you may not be so keen for Mrs. Oliver to hear you're calling on a lady with Mrs. Foster's reputation. Wives are women, they jump to conclusions, and you'll never make them understand that all you wanted was a change of female company. And mostly it wouldn't be true, anyway. If ' P ' really is married it's not surprising he's keeping in the background. No, the chap I want to lay hands on is the fellow who left the cigarette. I'm a lot more sure why he hasn't come forward. In his shoes I doubt if I would myself."

" Is there any proof the cigarette was left that night? "

" I think so. That house was like a show-piece, not a bit of dust, not a footprint, everything in the right place. The stub had been chucked down by some chap who's accustomed to having a slave clear up after him. We don't know yet who paid the rent. The landlord says it was paid monthly in treasury notes by Mrs. Foster in person. The last time she paid it, which was two weeks before she died, she intimated that she'd be leaving the house as she hoped to be getting married. She was a good tenant, not troublesome, never asking for repairs, rent paid on the nail, nothing against her except this Mrs. Fanshawe who lived opposite. Joe Fanshawe says she never troubled them and had a right to have friends if she wanted. He used to see her in the bar of an evening and he said the chaps were after her like bears after honey.

She didn't do a thing to attract them, just sat there and waited for them to come over. As they always did."

" There's the chap in the grey Bentley," Oliver suggested.

" Who could be the same one who paid the rent, though it doesn't seem likely to me. A chap who's been so discreet for five years that no one's prepared to identify him isn't suddenly going to advertise himself by a car you can't mistake."

The chap in the grey Bentley had not come forward either, of course, but you would hardly expect that, he would. If a chap wants to commit suicide what's wrong with the gas oven?

None of Stella's dressmaking clientele were able to help much. She had not been one for talking of her private affairs and none of them had ever been invited to the house. She had mentioned that she was probably moving quite soon and they had all regretted to hear it, because she was reliable and her charges were moderate. They usually paid in cash.

" And no Income Tax returns," reflected Davis. " That 'ud account for the fact that the payments never appeared in her bank account, where her sole income seems to be a small quarterly dividend inherited from her mother."

There had been a fair amount of money in ready cash on the premises when the police searched them. Further questioning convinced him that the man who paid the rent and was presumably Friday's visitor, and the owner of the grey Bentley, were two different people. And Mrs. Fanshawe, and what he'd have done without her at this juncture he frankly didn't know, recalled the Bentley's first visit on a Friday evening, after the regular visitor had gone. " Gone much earlier than usual," she added. She was full of speculations as to what might have taken place, but Davis cut her short, reminding her that all the police can handle is evidence. His own idea was that Friday's visitor had wanted to put paid to the account —perhaps his wife had found out or he had met a more glamorous blonde or discovered that the rising cost of living would not allow for expenses on the side on this scale—or simply felt he was getting past it. He had had the sense to leave nothing on the premises in writing and Davis thought on the whole he was more likely to be a widower or a bachelor than a married man. Every Friday night for five years was likely to strain the credulity of the most innocent wife.

There was the anonymous letter, of course, but the inspector had pinned that on to Mrs. Fanshawe; she had tried to play the part of the innocent, but he soon demolished her defences. Eventually he narrowed his suspects down to three—Friday's visitor, the owner of the grey Bentley and the anonymous Pete. The last sounded to him like a commercial, in which case he was pretty sure to turn up in the neighbourhood again, since these chaps normally followed a certain route. As to the other two, he could go on guessing for a month of Sundays and find himself where he started, like the Red Queen running like mad and never advancing a step. But he knew that, nine times out of ten, murderers deliver themselves to the rope. They lose their heads and betray themselves in a moment of panic. Or they become over-confident and drop a hint and someone picks it up. Or some third party stumbles on a clue or realises he has a bit of information that might be some use, and we all want to stand in well with the police. Patience be our watchword, decided Davis. Patience and the eye that never sleeps. Come to think of it, they are a policeman's capital assets.

" And how," Crook would have said if he could have heard the inspector shooting off his mouth. He also had seen the report of Stella Foster's death and recognised her from the photograph in the press.

" I could have told the narks that one was never destined to die in her bed of old age," he observed to Bill Parsons. " I wonder which of them it was—the chap who drove her into the Nell Gwynn, the one who drove her home again, or our dear old friend—A.N. Other."

CHAPTER VII

OTHERS BESIDES Crook had seen the news. In the Sumner household Gerald departed on the Thursday with the *Post*, leaving the local paper for Muriel. Muriel being busy about the house, it was Dot who first read of Stella Foster's death, and her shriek of horror brought her sister from the kitchen premises.

" What on earth's the matter, Dot? Have you hurt yourself? "

" Mu, come quickly. Shut the door and take a look at this." She extended the paper, folded, so that Stella's picture was uppermost.

" I haven't got my glasses," said Muriel rather crossly. " What is it? "

" Gerry's inamorata."

" Do be careful. Mrs. Hogg has ears a yard long. What's happened to her? Got herself murdered? "

" Yes," said Dot, flatly.

" I dare say she deserved it. Women like that . . ." Muriel came to a shocked fullstop. " You're not serious, Dot? "

" It was serious enough for her. It's all here. She was last seen alive on Tuesday. The woman across the road saw a man go in at eight-thirty. Gerry was late that night, remember. He said he was in London, but I . . ."

" You saw him at Pheasant Green at half past seven. I know. Well, that seems to prove he wasn't visiting this Mrs. Foster—is that her name?—at half past eight. He was home soon after nine, remember. Here," she ferreted in the pocket of her overall and produced a pair of spectacles. " Let me see. It says she was well-known in public houses and often took a man back with her. Well, there's your answer. She's taken one man home once too often."

" That won't be good enough for the police," prophesied Dorothy soberly. "They'll want to know the man's name. If they come asking questions . . ."

"I can't see any reason why they should, but if they do, Gerry was in London that night. He telephoned. The only time, so far as I know, he set eyes on the creature was that evening at the Nell Gwynn. As for the wristwatch, I made a fine fool of myself over that. Gerry had bought it for me. He gave it me last night. What else does the paper say?"

"She had a regular Friday night visitor . . ."

"Let the police find him and the odds are they've got their man. Even you aren't going to suggest it could be Gerry. We're always at the Nell Gwynn on a Friday."

"Mrs. Foster wasn't killed on a Friday."

"Whose side are you on, Dot? I tell you, I don't care if this woman was hacked into little pieces. I'm perfectly certain she only got what was coming to her, and I'm only sorry for whoever did it. But *Gerry isn't involved.* He was in London on Tuesday night. Go on saying that to yourself till you believe it."

"Are you suggesting you do?"

"It doesn't matter if I believe it or not. I'm on Gerry's side anyway." A new thought struck her. "Dot, I wonder if he's seen this. And I can't even telephone because it would look as though I wasn't sure."

Peter Garland drove his car into the parking- space at the Case Is Altered at Turnbury and wandered along to the commercials' room. An evening paper lay on the table and the first thing he saw in it was a picture of Stella Foster and a caption: WHO IS PETE?

"Police," he read, "are anxious to interview a man, giving the name of Pete, who was asking for Mrs. Stella Foster in two public houses at Martindale on the night of her death."

He dropped into a chair and read the report. Stella Foster had been found strangled, death had taken place on the evening of Tuesday, the 14th. A man had been seen to enter the house at eight-thirty and had not been seen to leave. Someone had been seen trying to get admission at nine o'clock. Neither man had as yet been identified. A man called Pete had been inquiring for the dead woman, and a card signed " P " had been delivered at her house by the first post on Wednesday.

After a while Peter Garland went into the bar and ordered a whisky-and-soda. " Had a bit of a shock," he confided to the barman. " Friend of mine, well, someone I know, say, has got herself murdered." He laid the paper on the bar.

" Asking for it," opined the barman, briefly. He shot the young man an odd look.

" She was all right," Garland retorted, instant in his defence of the dead woman. " No harm liking a bit of fun."

" Maybe you should be helping the police," suggested the barman.

" I was going to ask you the way to the station. This is a new round for me, haven't got my bearings yet."

The barman stopped mopping the counter. " You know something? "

" It was my postcard," said Peter Garland, gently. " No wonder I couldn't get any answer when I went round that night. Her nine o'clock visitor, remember, the one who couldn't get in." He passed his hand over his forehead. " I can hardly believe it now. She always seemed more alive than anyone else."

" You were asking the way to the station," observed the barman, pointedly.

Garland's head came up with a jerk. " You're not thinking . . . ? I didn't do it, you know."

" Anyone suggest you did? "

Garland laid some money on the counter and picked up his shabby raincoat. " I'll be getting along," he said. " Stella! My God, what a thing to happen."

At the station he wasted a little time explaining who he was; and when that point was cleared up he had to wait for a senior officer to be sent for. He explained that he hadn't come forward before because this was the first he had heard of the affair, and told them about the newspaper. In his subsequent statement he said:

" I didn't know Mrs. Foster very well. I met her some months ago at the Horn of Plenty. I pass through Martindale every two or three months and we happened to get into conversation. When the pub closed I asked if I could see her home, and she said O.K. I didn't go in with her, not that time, but I said if she was likely to be at the Horn the next night perhaps she'd come out with me somewhere. She was there and we left together, and got something to eat at a roadhouse. I have a car, of course, you have to in my job. She didn't want to go to the flicks or dance, so after dinner we went back to her place. She gave me a drink and then we started fooling about, having a bit of fun—you know. She was a good sport. She knew I was a married man, and she told me she was married, too, but not living with her husband. After that I generally saw her when I was in the district. I used to bring her little presents—nylon stuff mostly, that's what I travel in. I knew she had a regular friend— her Daddy I used to call him—she said that was all right, he only came on Fridays and the rest of her time was her own. That suited me, and as I say, we met whenever I was passing through. Mind you, she had other dates and sometimes she couldn't make it, but it wasn't serious on either side. I had no intention of breaking with my wife, and Stella—Mrs. Foster—knew it, but, well, she's with her mother in Wales with the kid most of the year, and I'm generally on my own, so—you know how it is."

The wooden-faced sergeant said nothing to that. In his opinion chaps who played around with hot pieces like Stella Foster had only themselves to blame if they got burnt. He listened with precious little comment to the rest of the young man's statement.

" I went to the Horn of Plenty first to see if she was there, because that's where we'd mostly met. Round about eight o'clock was her usual time, but of course she might have got delayed and I waited round for about twenty minutes. I asked the barman if he'd seen her, but he said

No, so presently I went along to the Coach and Horses. I knew she went there sometimes, though I'd never actually met her there. I talked to a chap who knew her, and he said she was at home, his wife had seen a friend go in. I'd brought her a little present and I didn't want to take it back with me, so about nine o'clock I drifted down Hallett Street and rang her bell. There wasn't any answer, and pretty soon I moved off again. Waste of a whole evening," he added, gloomily. " When I got back to my hotel they told me there'd been a telephone call just after I left, about half past six, from a chap who could put a nice bit of business in my way. I was browned off, I don't mind telling you. To miss my girl and a nice little thing on the side. I could do with the commission, too," he added, with a rueful grin.

" You weren't staying at Martindale, then, Mr. Garland? "

" Lord, no. A little place called Thirlbury, an eleventh-hour deviation. That's why I couldn't give Mrs. Foster any more notice. She hasn't got a telephone."

" And—you didn't try and get in touch next day? "

" I was off at eight."

" Or write? What about the present you were taking? "

" I've still got it. A rather nice nylon blouse, stand you up for about six pounds in the shops. She liked nice things."

The police officer's expression said unhelpfully, " Don't we all? " Really, the chap was about as sympathetic as a bulldozer. " The officer in charge of the case will want to see you, I expect," he said.

The young man moved uneasily. " My employers won't like it if I bitch up their round," he said. " I can hardly take it in even yet. Do they know when—I mean if it was that night? "

The sergeant said, " A chap went in at half past eight. If she lived alone it seems likely she opened the door. No one ever saw her alive after that."

" So that when I was pounding at nine o'clock—do they know when he left? "

" I dare say Inspector Davis can tell you that when you see him," responded the sergeant.

They made him wait while they rang up Martindale, and they typed out a statement for him to sign. Replying to some additional questions he said he hadn't seen anyone in the street, had not heard anything except the sound of Stella's wireless, which was kept on all day, he understood; but he did recollect almost cannoning against a man as he came up into the High Street.

" But he didn't come from Hallett Street," he insisted. " He came out of a side road." Then he stopped. " Wait a minute," he said. " There are back doors to those houses."

" You didn't see him come out of a back door? "

" I told you, I'd just reached the High Street. But—I suppose he could have done. I don't know where that road leads to anyway."

" Know him again? "

Garland looked scandalised. " On a wet night—a chap with his hat banged over his eyes getting out of the rain as fast as he could? What do you think? I suppose I've as much likelihood of recognising him as he of identifying me." He put his face in his hands. " Tell me this. Is all this going to come out? I mean, my wife . . . ? "

" You should have thought of that a bit sooner," said the sergeant.

Garland looked at him oddly. " You didn't know her, of course, Mrs. Foster, I mean. I wouldn't say she was a raving beauty, but there was something about her that you couldn't resist. I'd see other fellows watching her, and I knew they felt just the same as me. I'd say, if she'd put her mind to it, she could have married half a dozen chaps."

" No, she couldn't," retorted the humourless sergeant. " That 'ud be bigamy."

Eventually they let him go, after he had furnished authority with a map of his probable movements during the next few days. He was warned that he must be prepared to attend the inquest, if he was called upon, and advised not to deviate from his plans without giving the police notice.

The inquest on Stella Foster was held the next day; it was purely formal, evidence of identification and cause of death being taken. No relatives appeared and no one offered to accept responsibility for the funeral. Nor did any search of the cottage reveal the existence of a will. The verdict was wilful murder against some person or persons unknown, and the police inquiry went on. Peter Garland went home a day or two later to visit his wife and child, and was relieved to find that they had no interest in the late Mrs. Foster, though he knew that before long they might be ablaze with it. His mother-in-law had never cared for him, and now she would be able to justify her dislike.

" They don't seem to have cottoned on to Coppernob," observed Crook to his buddy, Bill Parsons. " Still, that's their headache, and who are we to provide the police with aspirins? "

All this while in his office at Beckfield Henry was on pins and needles, wondering which way the cat would jump. For the first time in his life he knew he was up against something that might easily prove too much for him, for he had learned from professional experience that it doesn't matter how careful you are, you can never guarantee that the truth won't emerge. It isn't enough to refrain from correspondence, to change your name, to cover up left, right and centre, there is always the Invisible Witness, the man against whom you cannot guard, because you don't know of his existence.

But in point of fact the Judas in this case was no stranger, but someone of whose potential ability to destroy him he should already have been aware.

The police were still hot on the scent, though the dead woman now lay underground, when Miss Bainbridge brought a cable into Henry's office.

This read:

"FATHER DIED SUDDENLY BURIED AT SEA RETURNING AT ONCE."

and it was signed: BEVERLEY CARR.

Miss Bainbridge put the message on the desk and stood meekly behind Henry's chair. But it didn't require Henry's silence, the look of petrifaction that sealed his features into immobility, to reveal the truth to her. She had known it long ago. At last he turned his head.

"Did you want . . . ? Oh, no answer, of course."

"No, Mr. Henry," said Addie in a voice of holy quiet, and glided away.

Henry clenched his hands on the bit of paper. Beverley his darling, he thought, his shining hope, for whom he would take any chances; Beverley within his reach at last and yet, perhaps, unattainable. It was like the melodramatic silent films of his boyhood, violence and what-have-you and then the caption: *Between them rose the spectre of a dead woman.* He laughed abruptly and Avery, coming in, looked at him with surprise.

"We've lost a client," said Henry.

"And is that amusing?"

"Not at all." What a stick the fellow was. "His daughter's on her way home. She may come here. If so, I want to see her."

"Are we handling the funeral?" asked Avery, obtusely.

"Seeing he died at sea, I should imagine not. A pity we can't all arrange to die so conveniently. All this ritual and fuss . . ." He looked up sharply to find an unwonted look on the young man's face. Clumsy, he reproached himself, mortified by his blunder. There wasn't much you could tell Avery about rough and ready burial. He had seen corpses pitched helter-skelter into pits and covered over by bulldozers, with no memorial and precious little reverence.

Avery put down the paper he had brought in and, when the question he had raised was settled, he went away, thinking, Old Uncle H. looked almost coy. Surely he can't be thinking of romance at his age. And then an unwilling grin split his face as he added, " All the same, I wouldn't put it past him, the old fox."

Another thirty-six hours elapsed before Inspector Davis's anticipations were justified. Patience and the eye that never sleeps, he had said. This time it was patience that brought home the bacon. Information was brought to him that a new witness was outside, with something to relate in connection with the Foster affair. The man gave his name as Saunders, and declared that he had additional evidence.

" Does he think evidence is an egg to be sat on till it's hatched? " demanded the inspector. " All right, I'll see him."

His reactions to Mr. Saunders were unequivocally unfavourable. He told himself he knew the type, potential criminals even if they never came into court, toadies, lick-spittlers, untrustworthy witnesses to boot. All the same, he composed himself to listen.

What Mr. Saunders had to tell him was of considerable interest. He identified the dead woman as being connected with one Mr. Browne who had utilised certain facilities he himself offered in connection with an accommodation address for correspondence. He knew nothing of this Mr. Browne outside this connection, and the letters he received were few and far between. They were, however, always in the same handwriting, all but one, that is, and were always sealed with pale blue wax. The postmark, he happened to remember, was Martindale. Here Mr. Saunders looked so much like a mixture of Shylock and Uriah Heep that the inspector wanted to hit him. As it was he only murmured, " Hard cheese! " meaning bad luck the envelopes were sealed.

" What makes you connect this Mr. Browne with Mrs. Foster? " he wanted to know.

" Didn't I say? She came in one evening, well, after-noon, really, saying she'd posted a letter to this Mr. Browne and it was a mistake and she wanted it back. I told her, naturally, that I couldn't tamper with the letters after they'd arrived, and she asked if I forwarded them on or if the people called for them. I told her it was all according. Anyway, there wasn't a letter for him that morning. She was just trying to find out who he was."

" Mr. Browne," said the inspector, obtusely.

" That's what he called himself, but if that was really his name then he'd been borrowing someone else's handkerchief. He pulled it out of his pocket one day when he was in my place and I saw a G embroidered on it, as clear as clear."

" P'raps his name was George."

" Henry," said Mr. Saunders, laconically. " Well, I don't suppose Browne is his right name, they don't generally use their own."

" You're wasted selling tobacco," said the inspector, pleasantly. " The police could do with a chap like you."

Mr. Saunders sent him a sharp, stealthy glance, but there was nothing to be read in the official's straightforward gaze.

" Well, anyway, I thought I ought to let you know."

" H'm." The inspector doodled a little more. " Never seen this Mr. Browne anywhere, outside your premises? "

" No, I can't say I ever did. Mark you, I'd know him again anywhere."

" Any special reason? "

" Well . . ." Mr. Saunders considered. " He was a gentleman," he offered at last. " Different, somehow."

" Never happened to notice which way he went after he left your place? "

" I've other things to do."

" Thanks for your help," said the inspector, but not as gratefully as Saunders had anticipated. " We appreciate your trouble, and, of course, if you should get a line on this Mr. Browne, we rely on you to get in touch with us right away."

The mystery regarding the authorship of the postcard

having been solved, the press were delighted when a new factor turned up to add sparkle to the case.

STRANGLED WIDOW MYSTERY
WHO IS MR. BROWNE?

they inquired eagerly. There was a suggestion, quite unfounded at the time, that he might be identified with Friday's visitor. Much publicity was given to the fact that he had collected a letter, presumably from Mrs. Foster, on the night she was killed.

Avery, escorted by the inexorable Mr. Smith, bought an evening paper on his usual evening stroll. When he read the name Mr. Browne he laid it aside and started doing mental arithmetic. The night of Mrs. Foster's death, he recalled, Henry had, by his own admission, been in Martindale. He said he had been visiting Will Lockyer in hospital, but it had been around ten o'clock when he turned up at the Castle, which made it a bit late even for a case on the open list. And hadn't he thought it rum from the start that a selfish old codger like Uncle H. should traipse out weekly over a period of years to alleviate the boredom of a man he had never known hitherto? Besides, he had another piece of information that convinced him that Uncle Henry and Mr. Browne were one and the same. So now—what? Tackle the police? or Uncle H.? Or keep your mouth shut and let the author-ities get on with it?

Henry, reading the same headline, realised in a flash why he had been convinced he had left a gate open somewhere. Of course. Mr. Saunders. He was cynically surprised that the fellow had not come to call on him rather than the police, but reflected that most likely he could not afford to fall foul of the law. If Henry was any judge, the chap had seen the inside of a prison before to-day. And then, of course, Saunders did not know his actual identity. Indeed, Henry had taken careful steps to make certain that he should not. All the same, he felt his heart quicken that evening when a knock fell on his door, and he went to open it, prepared for the police, even for some anonymous blackmailer, but certainly not for his nephew, Avery.

"Come in, my dear boy," he said. "Where's the dog?"

"I left him at home."

"I didn't know he ever let you stir out without him."

Avery looked solemn. "He doesn't come with me on business appointments."

"So you're here on business, though scarcely by appointment. My dear chap, must you look so like the public hangman?"

Avery started. "What on earth made you say that, Uncle Henry? As a matter of fact, I came to tell you that I know you're Mrs. Foster's Mr. Browne."

Henry nearly laughed, it was so reminiscent of the music-halls to which an unrepentant nanny had taken him as a boy.

"Mrs. Foster's Mr. Browne!" He composed himself. "Do take a chair. You make me nervous prowling about like that. And explain yourself."

"You've seen the evening paper? Of course you have, it's on the table there. So you know the police are looking for a man who used to visit Mrs. Foster under the name of Browne?"

"You can't have the same paper as I have. Mine merely says that information has been received about a man called Browne collecting letters at an accommodation address. Why they should imagine he's connected with Mrs. Foster . . ."

"It's all in the paper," said Avery patiently. "This man who gave the information identified Mrs. Foster as a woman who called asking about Browne . . ."

"My brothers are right," murmured Henry, "you'll never make a lawyer. In any case, why identify me with the chap?" He sounded unflustered but curious, which was the fact; he really did want to know.

Avery's reply was unexpected, indeed it almost took his breath away.

"Mrs. Lockyer. She knows you as Browne, too."

Henry took it pretty well. Avery had to admit that. And what a profile, like a hawk, like a Red Indian, pitiless in its economy of line. One thing, he was not giving anything away.

"When did you meet Mrs. Lockyer?" Henry asked.

"The day after I met you in the Castle I found myself in Martindale, and I asked at the post office if they knew anything of a Mrs. Lockyer who had just lost her husband. It was very simple. I went to see her . . ."

"What on earth for?" Henry was frankly astounded.

"To know if there was anything I could do, of course. I explained that my uncle used to play chess with him, and before I could say any more she said, 'Oh, you're Mr. Browne's nephew, then,' and she asked me in. Anyone connected with you would be *persona grata* there, she implied."

"Could you," murmured Henry, "contrive to look a little less staggered by the discovery?"

"She said," continued Avery, steadily, paying no heed to this plea, "how grateful she was to you for coming week in, week out, for five years, every Friday as regular as clock-work, apart from holidays, of course. That rang a bell—Friday, I mean—though I didn't connect up right away. But now I remember it was a Friday I met you in the bus . . ."

"You've an enviable memory," Henry congratulated him.

"Not at all. It was the day of your anniversary luncheon."

"So it was. So you put two and two together and made—how many? Ninety-six?"

"According to the papers—I don't, of course, know if it's all true—Mrs. Foster had a regular Friday night visitor over a number of years. Mrs. Lockyer also had a Friday night visitor over a number of years, a man who called himself Browne. Mrs. Foster and Lockyer . . ."

"My dear Avery," Henry pointed out, "you're not

talking to an imbecile child. I got there some time ago. You've deduced that the Mr. Browne who played cards with Will and the Mr. Browne who visited Mrs. Foster are one and the same, and that his real name is Henry Greatorex. Well, what are you waiting for? You're a good citizen, aren't you, and it's a good citizen's duty to help the police. Quite how you expect to prove your contention . . ."

"There's Mrs. Lockyer," Avery reminded him, woodenly.

"My dear boy, have all your years of experience taught you so little? Don't you realise that if Mrs. Lockyer had seen me drive a knife into Mrs. Foster's heart, she'd look the other way and know nothing?"

Avery walked across to the door. "You won't want me hanging about," he suggested. "I merely wanted to assure you that if I can be of any assistance . . ."

"What assistance did you think you could offer me?" Henry wanted to know. "Unless you had a false alibi in mind, and, speaking as a lawyer, I don't advise it. When I was a young man, Avery, one of the greatest K.C.s of our time—they were K.C.s then, of course—told me that a false alibi is a through ticket to the condemned cell. I don't know, I don't remember, I wasn't there, that's the wise man's defence. So, not being completely addle-pated, I don't know who killed Mrs. Foster, because *I wasn't there*. From which it follows that there's nothing for me to remember. Q.E.D."

But though he met his nephew in this assured fashion, he knew in his own heart that his danger was now very acute indeed.

"The fact is," he told himself when he was once more alone, "too many people know the truth about Mr. Browne. Saunders, Mrs. Lockyer, Avery—it must come out sooner or later. Oh, well." He remembered the advice he always gave his clients. "Don't cross your bridges till you come to them, and even then it's sometimes wise to take a chance and try to swim across." It was salutary to realise how much simpler it was to give advice than to take it.

The situation deteriorated rapidly during the next twenty-four hours. For Mrs. Lockyer had also bought an evening paper and seen that the hue and cry was out for Mr. Browne. Walking home with the *Gazette* under her arm she found herself thinking of the young fellow who had come round saying he was Mr. Browne's nephew, and asking her if she was all right. It was what you might expect, reflected Mrs. Lockyer, he would not come himself for fear of embarrassing her, but he sent this serious young man to find out if she was managing. She was managing all right, and so she told him. Will had been well known at the Legion, and she had never been a spendthrift. Besides, she had her health and she was not above sixty, good for a day's work and would not thank you to try to prevent her. Sitting about by yourself and remembering is a sure road to despair. No, she told the young man, thank his uncle for his kindness, but she did not want for anything. Then two or three days later she got the paper and read about the police wanting to get in touch with a Mr. Browne. She did not doubt for an instant that it was the same man, and at once she knew she had been snared in as prettily-baited a trap as you could wish for. She recalled that Mr. Browne had never mentioned a nephew, not to her or Will, and this young man who had seemed so serious and interested and asked so many questions had not, of course, been any relation to Mr. Browne. No, he was the police coming to snoop. She felt the good anger rise in her heart. Then, casting her thoughts back urgently, she wondered if she had said anything compromising about Will's benefactor. But her conscience was clear. Actually, there was nothing she could have said, since she knew nothing. And then a fresh consideration dismayed her. On those blessed Friday evenings that Mr. Browne's charity had secured for her she had spoken of him openly to her cronies, and was it not more than likely she had said something that might put them on the trail? She could not be certain, well, of course she could not. The cleverest man alive could not be expected to remember every idle word, in spite of what the Bible said about accounting for them at the last day. She did not disbelieve the Bible, of course, it was just a mistranslation or something. Even if you were a Christian you had to have some common sense. What she could not recall accurately was whether she had ever referred to Will's visitor by name, or had she contented herself by saying he was the gentleman who was so kind to her poor husband? It was Alice Watson she had in mind, Alice with a tongue a yard long, who would probably go nattering to the grave. There was one way she could find out, so, in her old black hat and brown coat, because she did not want to look conspicuous by wearing her new mourning, she went to Alice's place, pleading early closing as an excuse for wanting to borrow a bit of margarine.

Mrs. Watson was delighted to see her. " Come along, do," she exclaimed in welcoming tones, " we've just been talking about you and your Mr. Browne. Did you see to-night's paper, Martha? "

" What about the paper? " inquired Martha, deadpan, sedate as a funeral mute.

" It says the police want to find a Mr. Browne who was in Martindale every Friday. And seeing he came round for Will every Friday for years . . ."

" Why should they want to see Mr. Browne? I mean, what's Will got to do with them? "

" Don't you see, Martha? Your Mr. Browne is the same as the one that used to visit Mrs. Foster."

" Who says so? " inquired Martha, stolidly.

" It's not likely there'd be two coming roundabouts on a Friday. Just think of it, it only shows you never can tell, being so nice to Will and then going on to that woman. Of course, Will was just an excuse in case his wife or anyone asked questions. Talk about deceitful! Why, Martha, you're never going without the margarine? "

" I've just remembered, I shan't be wanting any to-night."

" But, Martha, you ought to go to the police . . ."

" The police? Me? "

" Of course. To tell them about your Mr. Browne. Even if you don't think it was the same one."

" If it's not the same one, why should I inconvenience him? Anyway, I don't know where he lives; and if he wants to get in touch with me, he can do it himself, can't he? "

But when she had freed herself from Alice Watson she went home quickly, and shut the door and put up the chain, a thing she never did as a rule. She had the feeling that half Martindale would be prowling round her front door this evening. Because in her heart she felt as sure as Mrs. Watson that her Mr. Browne was the one the police were looking for. Only—did he know it? and, if not, could she warn him? She knew Alice Watson, she wasn't going to keep a quiet tongue in her head, and even if she did not go to the police herself (and Martha would not put it past her), she would see to it they heard, and then they would come along to Burns Row.

It was later that evening that she remembered Avery's visit, and the card he'd left her, in case she wanted to get in touch. She found it where she had carefully put it away, and read it. Avery Greatorex, 27 Garden Road, Beckfield. The name Greatorex did not mean a thing to her. A quiet woman, tied by her husband's affliction, she had scarcely been ten miles from her home in twenty years.

CHAPTER VIII

MARTHA WENT over to Beckfield on the ten o'clock bus next morning, but when she reached Garden Road an inquisitive landlady told her that Avery had gone to business. Martha asked timidly if the woman knew where he worked, and the landlady stared and said, " Well, Greatorex, of course. Where do you suppose? "

Martha was too much intimidated to ask for the address, but she found the office without difficulty. She could scarcely ask for Henry, since he had chosen to meet her as Mr. Browne, so she asked for Avery instead. By now she had changed her mind about his being connected with the police. She produced the young man's card and explained that he had told her to call if she needed help, and her name was Mrs. Lockyer and it was about her husband, who had just died. The office had become used to Avery's clients, a rum bunch, they thought them, so they fetched Avery out with no hesitation at all. He took her into his own office, which was about the size of a mousetrap, a simile that he considered not inappropriate, and gave her a chair.

" Tell me how I can help you," he said, and she answered, " The gentleman, your uncle, that would be Mr. Henry Greatorex. I was wondering if I could see him, if it wouldn't be bothering him too much. I wouldn't want to be a nuisance after him being so kind."

When Avery took her into Henry's far more luxurious sanctum, her Mr. Browne came to meet her with hand outstretched. But his heart was repeating, over and over, " This is it. This is it. This is it."

Martha explained earnestly why she had come. " I know Alice Watson, she'll put the police on to me, and they'll come round asking questions, and I don't know what I should tell them."

" Oh, the truth," said Henry at once, and whatever he

104

might be feeling his face and manner were unchanged. " It's perfectly simple. Someone who told you his name was Browne came to play chess with your husband once a week. What's wrong with that? "

" Suppose they want to know if there was an address for an emergency? "

" It's still simple. I gave you a number in Hive Street."

" Then they'll know it's—that you're the one they're looking for."

Henry said, rather curiously, " Why did you come to-day, Mrs. Lockyer? "

" To warn you about Alice Watson. I felt it was the least I could do."

He thought, " How did she know where to come? Avery, of course." Aloud, he said, " You can't do me any harm by telling the truth, and you couldn't do yourself any good by attempting to conceal it. I promise you it's all right," he added, laying a kind hand on her arm.

" You're quite sure? I'll say anything you tell me."

" I believe you would. But you mustn't let yourself be upset. Just answer their questions. That's the best advice I can give you. And it was nice of you to come. I do appreciate the trouble you've taken."

" I suppose," he observed to Avery, after Mrs. Lockyer had taken her departure, " you told her who you were? So she knew where to pick up the trail. You're very like your father, Avery. He was a good fellow and wanted less for himself than any man I've ever known, but wherever he went trouble went, too."

" I'd better go," said Avery, dryly. (The conversation was taking place in Henry's office.) " In a matter of minutes you'll have convinced me that the whole set-up is my responsibility."

" Has it ever occurred to you," Henry inquired, " that it isn't the wasters who bring wars to pass, but the honest men wanting to put the world to rights? Their intentions are excellent, but the unfortunate thing is that by the time they've finished the job there's precious little world left to save."

Avery went away, smarting. It was absolutely typical of old Uncle Humbug, he reflected, his brow like a thundercloud, at a time when murder was in the air, to put the other fellow in the wrong.

Martha Lockyer was justified in her fears. Within a few hours of her return she found a policeman on her doorstep. She parried his questions as long as she could, saying she did not know anything about Mr. Browne, except that he was a friend of Captain Barber of the Legion (it was safe to mention him, seeing he had been dead these two years gone). She did not know where Mr. Browne came from or anything about his private affairs. He had come for Will, not for her; he had sat with Will at the hospital that night, no, she was not sure when he left, probably about eight o'clock. He had not come to the funeral, but she was not surprised, a busy gentleman like him, and he had sent lovely flowers.

Authority put an unerring finger on the weak spot. " How did he know your husband was ill? "

So she had to confess to the address in Hive Street.

" An accommodation address—not where he lived."

" I wasn't to know that."

" You never went to call on him there? "

Mrs. Lockyer was frankly scandalised. " You don't go troubling a gentleman who's been as good to you as Mr. Browne was to Will."

" And you don't know his real name? "

" Mr. Browne."

" Suppose I tell you that's not his real name? "

" It's the one he gave Will and me."

" Have you seen him since the funeral? "

" He didn't come to that, just sent flowers. Lovely they were. Will would have appreciated that. Always wished he could have a garden—my poor Will."

" And he hasn't been to see you ? "

" There was no reason."

" Or written? "

" No. And if he had," said Mrs. Lockyer in the same quiet voice, " I can't see how it would make any difference to anything you might want to know. Will and me were never in trouble with the police."

He could see he was making no headway there, and in any case he did not imagine there was anything she could tell him, so he let her go. He had other arrows in his quiver, and he could always come back to her, if need be. So he pursued his inquiries at the Martindale General Hospital, where he unexpectedly scored a bulls-eye. For, though the matron only knew Henry as Mr. Browne, Dr. Potter clearly recalled seeing him rush away on the night of Stella's death. Yes, he agreed, Matron had told him it was a Mr. Browne, and it was no concern of his how many names Henry cared to use, but he had no doubt at all that it had actually been Henry Greatorex. The time was about eight o'clock; he remembered that because the patient he had come to see had died at eight-thirty. His manner said it was very ungrateful after all his trouble.

" And don't ask me why he was calling himself Browne," he added. " I suppose there's no law against it. Anyway, he's in the legal racket himself, so he should know."

The immediate consequence of this was that twelve hours later Inspector Davis came to see Henry.

Henry received him very politely. He agreed that he was Mr. Browne, and had the good sense not to offer any explanation or excuses. As Dr. Potter had observed, there was no law against him calling himself anything he pleased when he visited his personal friends. Davis suggested slyly that perhaps he had adopted a false identity to prevent Mrs. Lockyer coming to pester him at his private address. Presumably he hoped to rouse Henry's dander by this, but Henry was not playing to that ball.

" I thought all the police had courses in psychology these days," he observed. " I understand you've seen Mrs. Lockyer? Well, then, you must realise she's not that type at all."

He could offer no confirmation of his story as to his subsequent movements, agreed that he had left the hospital about eight o'clock, had walked part of the way home, stopping for refreshment at a coffee stall. He did not imagine anyone there would remember him, and even if they did they would scarcely recall the time of his visit. He assured the inspector that he knew all about his legal rights, and when he wanted a lawyer present he would ask for one.

He made no attempt to deny his relationship with Stella, and answered questions with an unexpected candour. He acknowledged all those facts that it would have been folly to refute, but stuck to it that he had not seen Stella since the Friday evening when she told him of her husband's death and her own plans for the future. Yes, she had spoken of marriage. No, he could not supply the name of the prospective groom. He could offer no assistance in the matter of her friends; she had been free to make these as it pleased her. When Davis asked outright if there had ever been any suggestion of marriage between them, Henry replied that the thought had never been in his mind. Mrs. Foster had been a widow only a few days before their final meeting; there had never been any question of a divorce.

Davis refused to be diverted. " You say the notion of marriage was never in your mind, but Mrs. Foster had told her landlord that she expected to be leaving the house shortly and remarrying. In the circumstances, were you proposing to continue the relationship? "

" I was not."

Davis drew a bow at a venture. " You were perhaps proposing to end it, on account of a fresh attachment perhaps . . . ? "

Henry exploded. " My dear fellow, can't you talk English? A fresh attachment, indeed! What a gross expression. I can assure you I have nothing to add to what I have already said."

" There are still a few points on which we should value your assistance," returned Davis, coolly. " I understand that you collected a letter from Mrs. Foster at Hive Street on the afternoon of her death."

" I collected a letter."

" From Mrs. Foster? "

" You know as well as I do you can't put a non-existent letter into court," said Henry, gently.

" So you destroyed it? No doubt you had your reasons."

" I'm a lawyer," Henry reminded him.

" Do you refuse to divulge the contents of the letter? "

" I never realised till now that policemen do talk just like characters on the radio," commented Henry. " No, I don't deny its existence, and I don't refuse to repeat the contents. Mrs. Foster said she would be glad to see me any time I cared to drop round. Those are not precisely her own words, but by and large the letter was an invitation."

" And you accepted it? "

" Aren't you forgetting," asked Henry, softly, " that she met her death that evening? "

" No." Davis was blunt to the point of violence. " I'm a policeman, sir. My job is to find out who visited Mrs. Foster that night and strangled her."

" Aren't you inclined to put the cart before the horse? " Henry was fully in control of himself again. " Surely you have to get the facts and then formulate a case, not formulate a charge against a certain person and then see if the facts can't be squeezed in to suit your pattern."

" You've no right to say such a thing, Mr. Greatorex. My job, as I said before, is to find the murderer of this wretched woman. I know you had a letter from her that afternoon. You say you didn't visit her. But you didn't answer the letter, either."

" No correspondence ever passed between Mrs. Foster and myself."

" Then you intended to ignore her letter? "

" I can't remember telling you that, Inspector."

" If you didn't know she was dead, why did you make no move to see her? "

" My regular day had been Friday for a period of

years. I'm a man of method, as lawyers tend to be . . ."

" So you intended to visit her on Friday? "

" I didn't say that either. Before Friday came round I'd heard the news that she was dead."

Davis began to stiffen. " You say, Mr. Greatorex, that you normally visited her on a Friday. But there was nothing to prevent your visiting her on any other day, I take it? "

" Only her possible convenience."

" You were in Martindale that evening."

" Visiting the hospital. Did Saunders mention that there was also a letter from Mrs. Lockyer that afternoon? "

" It's unfortunate," suggested Davis, " that you can produce no witness of your movements after leaving the hospital."

" A mutual misfortune," agreed Henry, cordially. " You have no witnesses that I was in Hallett Street."

He extinguished his cigarette and drew out his case.

" Thank you, sir," said Davis at once.

Henry's brows lifted, but he held out the case with a murmur of apology. Davis bent over to accept a light. When he was well away he continued, " Did you know that Mrs. Foster owned a revolver? "

" She showed it to me. I understand it had belonged to her husband, and since she never used it she had no licence for it. If you are thinking, Inspector, that she threatened to kill me, I can assure you you're mistaken." His smile would have charmed a hippopotamus out of its pond during a heat wave. But Davis had even more resistance than a hippopotamus.

" What made her produce it at all? "

" She was telling me about Sydney Foster's death and said she had been going through such possessions of his as she still had, and the revolver was among them. I'm not an expert on firearms but I should assume that after a period of disuse, running into years, a revolver would be rusted or clogged or rendered ineffectual in some way."

" You know that the revolver was found on the floor close to the settee? " Davis offered.

"There was a statement to that effect in the press."

"So it looks as though she had produced it again."

"Perhaps she showed it to all her visitors in turn," Henry suggested.

Davis thought that, if Henry had been the corpse and Stella the accused, any counsel worth his salt could have got her off on a plea of extreme provocation. Henry gave him no more change during the remainder of the interview. Like Crook, he knew that the police cannot disprove statements you have not made. All the same, the last laugh was with the inspector. When he departed he took with him a partially-smoked cigarette, secreting it in his pocket while Henry was politely opening the door. Since no mention of the stub found in the dead woman's house had appeared in the press, Henry had no notion of his own peril. Not that he was fooled. He knew Davis was out to make a case against him, if he could. His best hope was to say as little as possible; but he had reckoned without the cigarette. When the inspector called on him the next day and asked him to explain the presence of the stub in the hall, since, on his own showing, he hadn't been inside 17 Hallett Street for a month, he saw hope drop dead at his feet. The tobacconist who made these cigarettes had been rumbled and compelled to give evidence. Even Henry could find no reply to that one. He walked out of his office as cool as a sea-breeze, but he had all his wits about him, knew that the fellow lounging on the farther side of the road had been put there by the authorities after Davis's first call, in case he (Henry) thought of putting in a few days in Brighton or taking a plane to the Continent. At the corner a car met them, and he stooped his tall head and got in.

That night Beckfield was electrified and infuriated to learn that Henry Greatorex had been detained by the police in connection with the Foster murder.

It was not only in Beckfield that the sense of shock penetrated. Up in London the brothers were paralysed by the news.

" It seems so out of character," exclaimed Charles Greatorex. " I don't mean keeping a woman—there was never anything of the monk about Henry, and with unmarried men of his age it's generally one thing or the other—but getting involved in a scandal of this sort. All the same, if what you tell me about Beverley Carr is the fact, it makes the affair a possibility. There was always a streak of recklessness in Henry; we've been fortunate that he's kept it under until now."

Richard agreed. " Henry was always one of those fellows you can push and push and he never turns on you, too polite or too lazy, you can take your pick. But then comes the one push too many. Should we act for him or would it better to leave the defence to outsiders? We shall have to consider counsel, too. Platt-Douglas might be our man. They say he's won acquittals when the hangman was already measuring the drop." He saw the crease of distaste in his brother's forehead and exclaimed, in more normal tones, " Great heavens, Chas, I still can't take this in. Henry—arrested for murder."

" You could rely on Henry to blow up on a large scale. He'd never be run in for petty fraud." Charles's voice was bitter with disappointment; until now he had not realised how much affection his half-brother had commanded in his own heart. " The fact is, Rick, neither of us has ever had Henry's true measure. We're like the rest of the world, diddled by a very smooth exterior and enormous charm of manner. Beneath that, he may have been a murderer in essence for the past twenty years, for all we know to the contrary."

The office door opened and Avery stalked in. He looked as grave as the Day of Judgment and as pale as a ghost.

" It's about Uncle Henry's defence, sir," he began, exactly as though he were in command of the situation. " It 'ud be too awkward for the family to represent him (he brushed aside Richard's stately, My brother and I have been considering that) and it's no use getting a penny-in-the-slot lawyer. This is an out-of-the-run case.

112

An ordinary well-meaning chap isn't going to be any use here."

" To hear you talk," exploded Charles, " one might suppose you thought your uncle guilty."

" I don't know that he isn't, sir." Avery was perfectly unmoved. " I question if, at bottom, you're absolutely sure yourself." The two elderly men looked paralysed as their nephew swept on, " I've known for a long time that Uncle H. was a surprise packet, and the police don't make such an unpopular arrest unless they've a pretty strong case. Most of Beckfield doesn't care a flip of the finger if Uncle H did it or not; they regard it as *lése-majesté* to lay a finger on him."

" Are you suggesting we shall connive at any attempt to—er—cook the facts? " inquired Richard, bluntly.

" Shall we say—arrange them to the best advantage? " murmured Avery. " Isn't that our job in any case? It's established that he was in Martindale on Tuesday evening, visiting a dying man in hospital. Further than that, he won't commit himself, but, speaking personally, I'm pretty sure where he was. He came into the Castle Hotel at Beckfield about ten o'clock; he was seen to leave the hospital two hours before. Where did he spend those two hours? No one ever saw him walking more than the distance from his flat to his office for the good of his health. Now, Uncle Rick, don't bawl me out till you've heard what I've come to say. I know a man who might be able to help, because he's like the kid in the film, will never take No for an answer. His name's Crook, Arthur Crook . . ." He stopped, at the sight of their angry, incredulous faces. For an instant they looked as alike as Tweedledee and Tweedledum.

" My dear Avery, I find it difficult to believe you would make a jest of the occasion. Our firm has always stood very high in the profession. We should scarcely wish to court *more* adverse publicity by allying ourselves with a fellow of that kidney. A *mountebank*," he added, in forceful tones.

" Actionable, Uncle Rick," Avery warned him, still

unsmiling. Really, the fellow was more like Henry than they had believed possible. " In point of fact, I wasn't thinking of the firm. I was thinking of Uncle Henry. Crook can't only make himself believe black's white, he can hypnotise other people into believing it, too, and that's the sort of chap we want. I've got a nodding acquaintance with him, I could drop round and have a word."

" It's not to be thought of," began Richard, but Charles interrupted, though with obvious reluctance, " Avery may have something there, Rick. Of course, I know the fellow's reputation as well as you do, he'd not only swallow the camel, he'd swallow the driver as well."

" You see," continued Avery, quite unmoved, " the great advantage of Crook is that it won't be anything to him whether Uncle Henry did strangle this woman or not. His job is to get an acquittal or prepare the ground for counsel to work for one, and, if he's persuaded that Uncle Henry didn't do it, then the odds are it'll never come to a trial at all."

" I must say, sir," exploded Richard, " your principles leave a good deal to be desired."

" Oh, principles! " Avery shrugged faintly. " They're a matter of experience, expediency even. I can't see any sense in throwing good money after bad. You can't bring this woman back to life, so why expend Uncle Henry as well, and incidentally make a good many people pretty miserable? "

Before either of the brothers could make any comment on that, there was another interruption. The door was opened sharply and a girl came spinning into the room. She was rather short, very delicately made, and quite beautiful, with that bloom on hair and skin that belongs only to youth.

All three men swung round at sight of her. She stopped short, her grey eyes widening.

" Oh! I didn't know you were engaged. I thought . . ." She looked from one to the other but it was on Avery that her glance lingered.

Richard came forward, one beautifully-kept hand outstretched.

" My dear Beverley, it's of no consequence. We were unable to write when we heard the sad news of your father's death, but you know you have our deepest sympathy."

" It can't be true," cried the girl, as though she had not heard a word. " All the way here I've been telling myself that. It's some hideous nightmare, isn't it? The police must have taken leave of their senses."

" The police? " Richard seemed aghast, but before either he or his brother could say another word Avery murmured, almost as though the matter were of no consequence, " I think, Uncle Rick, Miss Carr is referring to Uncle Henry."

" Well, of course," said the girl. " You . . ." She paused expectantly.

" This is our nephew, Avery," said Charles, quickly. " He works in the Beckfield office."

" Then you'll know it's a criminal mistake," cried Beverley Carr.

" Oh, it's that all right," agreed Avery. " The question is—whose mistake? As a matter of fact, we were talking about Uncle Henry just before you came in."

" Naturally, you know Henry didn't do it," she assured them. All three felt less disposed to believe in Henry's innocence than they had been five minutes before. Beverley, at least, had no compunction about wearing her heart on her sleeve, and for such a girl a secret romantic like Henry might be capable even of murder. Even as a boy Henry had had little sense of property, would let his most cherished possessions pass into other hands with little demur, but on those few occasions when he had set his heart on something, no matter how trifling it might appear to others, he had been inflexible. And if he wanted Beverley Carr, as they all were convinced he had, and this Mrs. Foster stood in his way, his odd code might even have assured him he had the right to protect their mutual happiness at any cost. Not that

115

that was the kind of argument even an outsider like Arthur Crook could put up to a jury.

" My dear, it is a most unhappy situation," said Richard, who could never quite shed his formality except to his brother. " But naturally we are leaving no stone unturned . . ."

" I hope you're digging them all out to throw at the police," said Beverley, stormily.

Avery's face quickened. " You can rely on Beckfield as a whole to do that," he promised.

The brothers frowned. Avery was as irresponsible as his uncle, their expressions declared.

" You are staying with your aunt in Curzon Street, I dare say? " Richard suggested, and once again Avery jumped in before anyone else could speak.

" If you've nothing better to do, will you let me take you out to lunch? I'll tell you all I can, but even I can't tell you whether he did it or not."

She drew a deep breath; it was like someone who has been haring along a dark road and is suddenly comforted by the sight of a resurrected moon. She couldn't be at ease with these old men, but with Avery she was instantly at home.

" Thank you, Avery." (The brothers gasped at the familiar address; Avery didn't even notice it.) " I'd like that."

Avery put a casual hand on her elbow and guided her out of the room. The brothers exchanged glances.

" Youth calling to youth," said Charles, with a sigh for days long gone by, so far off they were part of another world.

Richard was frowning still. " That boy'll never make a lawyer," he prophesied. " Nothing interests him but lost causes, and no successful legal practice can be built up on those."

Arthur Crook could have told him different.

CHAPTER IX

" I OUGHT to say," remarked Avery, leading the way to an eating-house where, he said, you could rely on getting a good cut from the joint, " how sorry I am about your father. It must have been a fearful shock, if you didn't know he was ill."

" I didn't. But it was merciful really from his point of view. He'd have been an invalid all his days if he hadn't had this fatal attack, and how he would have hated it. And so should I, in his place. Avery, don't let's talk about him. It's Henry who matters now. You don't really think he could have done it? "

" I wouldn't care to bet on it," returned Avery, candidly. " The longer you're with Uncle H. the less you seem to understand him. There's no doubt about their relationship during the past five years, and he doesn't deny it. But that's not a criminal offence and it's Uncle Henry's personal affair. The point the police are trying to make is that he had reasons for wanting to put an end to the situation." He sent her a candid glance. " Any help there? "

" I don't know," replied Beverley, matching candour with candour. " He must have seen he had only to lift his little finger and I'd come running. But then I'm only one of an army who'd probably do the same."

" I doubt whether Uncle Henry would acknowledge the army's existence." A waitress appeared and he gave the order without consulting his companion. " There's something you should bear in mind, Beverley, and that is that it's often more difficult to break that sort of relationship, which has no legal safeguards, than to get out of the marriage tie. Particularly if you're a romantic twenty-four hours a day, as he is, for all his worldly airs."

" Don't you like him? " asked Beverley, simply.

" The rum thing is," confessed Avery, " I'm cut to bits

about this. And I never expected to be. I've always thought of him as a lazy old buster—I'm sorry, but you did ask—crammed with charm—and it comes as a shock to me to realise how much it does matter that things shall go the right way for him. How long have you known him? "

" I met him nearly six months ago, but I had the feeling I'd known him much longer than that. If anything happens to Henry, Avery, I shan't be able to bear it. And the awful thing is I don't really know if I matter to him at all."

" Now, look," said Avery kindly, passing her the mustard as the waitress set down their plates, " Uncle H. has got himself involved in a murder case. You don't do that, particularly if you're H. G., unless you've got a good deal at stake. After all, he'd been doing very nicely, thank you, for five years. Why upset the apple cart now? Obviously because something's come along so important you can't dodge it. More, I was there when your cable arrived. He only said he wanted to see you, if you came in. There was no need to say more. If I'd known about Mrs. Foster and she'd proposed to stand in Uncle Henry's way, I'd have shaken in my shoes for her. Rather involved," he added hurriedly, " seeing I knew nothing of her till after she was dead. But you get my meaning. All the same, Beverley, take my tip and play it down. Crook's a bit of a wizard and more than a bit of a queer customer, according to some of our leading lights—Uncle Rick, for instance—but even he's going to find it a tough nut to crack if you hand him a first-class motive for Uncle Henry to want Mrs. Foster out of the way."

" But he wouldn't need to murder her," protested Beverley.

" There's something called blackmail, that can be both unpleasant and practically permanent."

" But what could she do, except threaten to tell me about them? "

" And it wouldn't have made any difference? " Avery looked at her curiously.

" I'm twenty-four," said Beverley. " I never imagined I should be the first woman in Henry's life. It would be almost too good to be true that I should be the one he wanted to marry. That being the case, how could Mrs. Foster hurt me? "

" I've seen too much of men in captivity to underrate what they have to endure," exclaimed Avery with unwonted passion, " but at this moment I could envy Uncle Henry. Oh, Beverley, stay out of the limelight. They'll be after you like greyhounds after an electric hare and that's the one thing that will drive Uncle Henry loco. Crook will tell you the same," he added.

" I'll do whatever's best for Henry, of course. Avery, there's one thing you must understand. Nothing will change my feelings towards him. If he did kill her—I know he didn't, but even if he had—it would only show he does care, and how much. And if he didn't, then he needs his friends now as never before, and come what may I shall always be his friend. Don't worry about publicity for me, because I don't care. I only want to do what will help him. And don't be moved by my aunt. She'd perjure herself black and blue to keep our name out of the papers. But, if things go wrong for Henry, my life won't be worth any more than his, and if they go right I could even bear to lose him—I think."

Avery left her on her doorstep and went along to the bus stop for Bloomsbury Street, where Crook had his office. He had passed through a number of experiences in his twenty-eight years, but losing his heart to a woman, so that nothing else mattered, was not one of them. He had been gracefully involved once or twice, but always with the knowledge that, if it came to a choice between her and his work, the woman would go to the wall. He had not, in short, hitherto believed in a world well lost for love. Now, having met Beverley, he began to wonder whether, for such a girl, a world might not be worth losing.

It was part of Crook's policy never to be surprised at

anything, so when a tall serious young man called Greatorex came to his office with a story of an uncle on trial for the Mystery Widow Murder he didn't whoop with excitement or say Kismet! or Another Hunch Come Home or anything melodramatic of that kind. He only asked, " What does this uncle of yours look like? "

When Avery had described him, finding it surprisingly difficult to " get over " Henry's personality, Crook said cheerfully, " Well, that's not the chap I had in mind. Know anyone with chestnutty hair, a regular Coppernob, married, prosperous, dashing with the ladies and drivin' a grey Bentley? "

" No," said Avery.

" Really? " returned Crook. " Take my word for it, the dear departed did. And I'll tell you something else. Unless the police have got him up their sleeves, which don't seem likely, he's keeping pretty carefully out of the picture." When he had heard what Avery had to say, he asked in the same undaunted voice, " Has your uncle been prepared? Well, no matter. I better go along and see him and find out what we can cook up."

Henry, that idle creature, had not lifted a finger to get a lawyer to defend him or given much thought to the question of counsel. With two brothers and a nephew in the profession, he felt he might safely leave such matters to them. All his thought was for Beverley and how to keep her name out of the case. Now he thanked his stars that he never had spoken of his hopes to any man. He did not believe his brothers had any idea how the land lay. Graham Carr was dead. There were no letters to link them in the public mind. Counsel would look for a motive, but in such a situation this would not be hard to find. Blackmail would be assumed and blackmail, in short, was the truth of the position between them at the time of Stella's death. If she had not uttered that fatal threat concerning Beverley he would never have paid that final visit.

When Crook came marching in, as hearty as a Victorian

curate at a church bun-fight, Henry was too startled not to show it.

"Introduce myself," offered Crook buoyantly. "Actin' for the defence—your defence." And then, as Henry remained speechless, he added courteously, "Not buttin' in, I hope?"

"My dear fellow, you must excuse me." Henry came to hurried and apologetic life. "First intimation I ever had my brothers have a sense of humour."

"Not your brothers," Crook corrected him. "The young fellow with the outlandish name."

"Avery? My nephew. I might have guessed. Ah, well, you're birds of a feather, aren't you?" (Though Heaven knew, their plumage could scarcely have been more dissimilar.) "Both out for lost causes."

"My causes," Crook told him, unwontedly frosty for the moment, "soon get themselves found once I'm on the scene. Now, how say we start with Chapter One, and remember, I'm not fussy. You don't have to do any editin' for my benefit. I'll do the editin' when the time comes."

"I take it you've seen the statement I made to the police, or at all events know what it contained."

"That's what I mean by editin'. I'll have the un-expurgated version. I'm not askin' you if you killed the lady, because bein' my client you have to be innocent, but it could help if you could say she was wavin' the little gun in your direction. Any man's allowed to act in self-defence."

"I doubt whether even you could swing that," Henry warned him frankly. "Mrs. Foster wasn't shot, she was strangled."

"Might make a chap see red if his hostess suddenly produced a lethal weapon?" Crook offered.

"Not in my case. I'd seen it before that night, you know."

"In your shoes I'd have stayed away the first time," Crook told him, to which Henry murmured that pre-sumably they didn't take the same size.

"Miss Carr come into this?" Crook hazarded, and Henry came to sudden violent life.

"Not if I can prevent it," he said.

"You can't," Crook assured him. "What with her and young Avery, you ain't going to have any chance of committin' suicide. And don't give me the story about not being there that night. You were there all right, and that's no crime. Go straight from the hospital?"

"I arrived about eight-thirty," said Henry. "I had a key but I didn't use it. I didn't need to, the door was on the latch. I pushed it open and realised Mrs. Foster was at home. There was a light on in the sitting-room and the wireless was playing. She had been expecting someone, so much was obvious, from the clothes she was wearing and the whisky she'd put out. She never touched the stuff herself. Only—it wasn't me she had been waiting for, and whoever it was had come—and gone."

"Meaning she was dead when you arrived?"

"Meaning just that. You didn't know her?"

"Just ships that pass in the night, but the little I saw was enough to convince me she'd founder off some reef before she reached harbour. No idea who it might have been, the chap she was all dolled up for?"

"I'm afraid I can't help you there. I dare say she had a number of visitors besides myself."

"You've got the police with you. Trouble is she never seems to have pin-pointed any of the others. Touch anything?" Henry shook his head. "Didn't open any drawers? Turn over the papers on the writing-desk? Nothing to indicate that there'd been someone before you?"

"She was dead," said Henry sharply. He remembered how she'd looked—afterwards. "She couldn't have done that herself."

"I meant something we could tie on to some other fellow—no classy spray of orchids, for instance? No bit of jewellery you hadn't seen before?"

"No, nothing like that. Only the newspaper, and I don't imagine the police——"

" What's that about a newspaper? " demanded Crook. " First I've heard of it."

" I suppose they took it for granted that it was hers. As a matter of fact, I could have told them that Mrs. Foster never took an evening paper, and she certainly wouldn't have gone out on a wet night to fetch one. Funny thing, I haven't given that paper a second thought, but surely, Crook, that's proof that someone had gone in before I did. It was much too late after I left the hospital to hope to pick up a paper, and I dare say Mrs. Lockyer would remember I didn't bring one with me." A new hope sparkled in Henry's grey eyes.

" You haven't got there yet," said Crook, patiently. " From the police point of view, the paper don't exist. You made a mistake there. You should have left it on the premises."

" I? I never touched it. It was there when I left the room."

" Then someone came back a bit later and removed it, because it wasn't there when the police broke in next day. I don't carry any flags for the boys in blue, but they wouldn't have overlooked a thing like that."

" I don't suppose it's very important," murmured Henry, absently.

" Not important? Upon my Sam, it's lucky for you you're a family business, or you'd be singing outside the pubs for your supper. Don't you see that's the first wisp of straw you've given me? "

" Straw? "

" Yes. For makin' bricks. Without bricks we can't hope to build up any foundation, and, though I can go into the brick business with as little straw as any man livin', even I can't do without it altogether. Go on, tell me more about the paper. Remember which it was? "

" The *Gazette*. The *Record*, which is the only alternative evening paper we can get, is a different shape, smaller . . ."

" Remember the headline? Or . . .? "

" Something about a railway accident, a fair number of fatalities."

Crook sent him a piercing glance. " Any special reason
you should recall that? I mean, here was your girl-friend
with the life choked out of her . . ."

" That's precisely why. So much death in the papers
that would be forgotten within a few days at most, and
one death in the same room that would fill the papers for
weeks to come."

Crook considered the point and nodded. " Could be,"
he agreed. " Well, don't you see where that gets us?
X, not knowing about your visit, remembers the paper
and comes back to look for it. Don't it seem that way
to you? No one else 'ud know it was there."

" It sounds somewhat far-fetched," Henry suggested.
" One newspaper's remarkably like another."

" That's what you think. But—say the owner had
started doin' a crossword, and used green ink? Or had
torn a bit out and kept that bit and showed it to someone
else, who might remember it afterwards. Or it might
have been delivered locally and have an address or an
initial. Oh, suppose half a hundred things. Any one of
them might be true. Well, let's have the rest of it. What
next? "

Henry described his flight by the back door, his pause
in the dark lane, like the City of Dreadful Night, he said,
his stealing past the shuttered houses . . . He told it
rather well. Crook hoped uneasily he would not tell it too
well in the witness box assuming he got so far. The
trouble was that he didn't know how he was going to
convince the police that this particular copy of the *Gazette*
had ever existed. Henry saw that difficulty.

" I realise you can't build much on a vanished newspaper," he said.

Crook stuck out a pugnacious jaw. " You can, if your
name's Arthur Crook. Pity you didn't think of it earlier.
Didn't case the joint, I suppose? "

" If you mean, did I examine the house—no? "

" So X could have been on the premises all the time,
heard you comin' up the path, made himself scarce, and
when you'd gone come beetlin' back for the paper . . .

Lucky for him there wasn't a telephone on the spot; you might have rung the police right away."

" I was concerned not to advertise my presence there," Henry pointed out. " My motive was pretty obvious."

" So could some other chap's have been. A dame who'll bring out a gun on the smallest provocation could have quite a number of enemies."

He asked a few more questions, then reached for his hideous brown billycock and rose to go.

" I'm sorry I can't be of more assistance to you," apologised Henry.

" If you can't have what you like, you must like what you have," Crook assured him. " I'm used to gettin' my effects with a rag and a bone and a hank of hair. Now, wait for our next thrillin' instalment and get yourself a bit of beauty sleep meantime. You look as if you could do with it. Oh, and your girl sent her love and young Avery's keepin' all the odd angles covered. There's the chap for my money," he added, enthusiastically. " Don't let a little thing like the letter of the law stop him gettin' results. Oh, take my word, one way and another the police are goin' to have a fine headache over this, and that's the way I like it to be."

" Your uncle doesn't do things by halves," he acknowledged candidly to Avery the same evening. " He's got himself into a very nice jam, and how we're goin' to show he didn't do it without producin' the one that did, beats me. Y'see, he admits now he was there that night, but swears someone else beat him to it. Which is what you'd expect," he added, calmly.

He recounted the latest version of Henry's story.

" Any proof, " asked Avery dryly.

Crook told him about the newspaper.

" He's taken his time remembering that," was Avery's grim rejoinder. " I mean—he didn't mention it to the police, did he? "

" According to him, he didn't think of it."

" You have to hand it to Uncle Henry, he's a cool card. Why didn't he think of it? Just forgot about it? Or . . ."

" Or didn't realise it might provide him with a way out? I give you two guesses which answer the police 'ull choose. You can hardly blame 'em. Line of least resistance and all that. All the same, we're going to pin this on to someone else, if I have to fake the evidence myself."

" And our next step? " questioned Avery, reflecting that it wasn't really hard to understand his brothers' prejudice against their nephew's choice.

" Our first job is to identify Coppernob. Doing anything this evening? Then come down and have a wee doch-an'-doris at the Nell Gwynn."

The doch-an'-doris, in effect, proved to be an excellent steak cooked to a turn and what the Nell Gwynn called French fried potatoes and Crook called chips. The manager, who knew his job, circled the room making sure his clients were satisfied.

" Give you a testimonial any time," Crook offered. " Matter of fact, I was rather hoping to see the fellow who recommended this place to me. Dines here often, I understand. Redhead, brings his wife—striking-looking chap, you may recall him."

" You mean Mr. Sumner? " suggested the manager. " As a rule he's here on a Friday, we don't see much of him in between. He lives out at Pheasant Green."

" That's the one," said Crook, cheerfully. " Drives a grey Bentley. Fridays, you said. Well, well, next time we're in the neighbourhood on a Friday we'll give you a hail."

" What a nice, obliging man," he cackled to Avery, when the manager had passed on. " Well, we're one step nearer home, but we've still a long way to go. Y'see, we might prove he knew the dear departed and even get him to admit it, but that don't say he murdered her. First thing is to find out where he was, according to himself, the night she died."

Avery said, with real curiosity, " How do you go about that? Just ask him? "

" Stringing me? " suggested Crook pleasantly. " No.

This is where we copy the palmist who looked to the hills for help. Not that I'm fussy where it comes from. It can pop out of the ground like a mole for me. *And* I don't care what it wears."

It wore, in fact, a long unfashionable coat and a hat with a wreath of flowers round it, and it delighted Crook's heart at first sight. When Bill Parsons pushed his head through the door of Crook's office and said, " A lady without an appointment in connection with the Foster case," Crook said cheerfully, " Never keep a lady waiting," and got to his feet as the door opened wider and Addie Bainbridge walked in. Crook breathed a delighted sigh. He placed her at once, one of those Rum Old Girls who could be depended on to stay any course, wouldn't let themselves be flummoxed by silly legal quibbles, and knew their story was the truth because they told it. " What's law but a lot of silly rules made up by men to suit themselves? " one of Addie's spiritual sisters had once demanded. And how should he disagree? He had never allowed them to cramp *his* style.

He looked at her affectionately, believing himself to be the man who had put the British spinster on the map. There they were, up and down the country, in their unobtrusive clothes and their unpainted fingernails, walking their dogs and buying the fish for their cats, often poor, always hard-working, sometimes patronised—and he wouldn't have changed them for a troupe of ballerinas.

He saw at once that Miss Bainbridge was going to be his cup of tea, hot, strong and sweet.

" It's exceedingly kind of you to see me without an appointment," she assured him in her sedate fashion, " but the truth is there is no time to be lost. I came straight up, I didn't even stop to tidy myself . . ."

" You look a treat," Crook assured her, meaning every word of it, " and it makes a nice change to see a hat that don't have to blush for itself."

Addie looked startled but gratified. Secretly she liked the hat herself, though it was only last year's furbished up with a new flower wreath, roses and forget-me-nots and a blue velvet bow instead of marguerites and buttercups and a black satin one. It sat fair and square on her forehead, making no concessions to whimsy or archness.

" Mr. Avery gave me the afternoon off," she explained, " but I thought it wisest not to mention I was coming to see you. Things do get about so in an office."

" Meanin' you work at Greatorex's. So you know my client."

" I have been Mr. Henry's secretary for years. The most considerate employer I ever had, for I know a young girl would be quicker."

" The hare was quicker on its feet but it lost the race," Crook encouraged her. " Henry Greatorex and me both like tortoises best."

" He calls me his right hand—his little joke, of course —but, Mr. Crook, he didn't do it. He didn't do it."

Crook looked pained by her ardour. " Well, of course, he didn't do it, sugar. I'm representin' him, ain't I? And my clients are always innocent. Any special reason for thinkin' he didn't? "

" I don't say he couldn't kill someone—there's a great deal more *to* Mr. Henry than young men like Mr. Avery realise—but not that way. He has beautiful manners," she wound up.

It was the kind of argument that would have made Henry's brothers stare uncomprehendingly—women and their logic, they would have agreed—but it seemed to Crook an excellent piece of deductive reckoning. Mind you, he knew he could not bring that sort of reasoning into court, but it proved to him that Addie Bainbridge knew her onions. Had Stella been shot or even poisoned he might have had his doubts but—Henry was a gentleman, he had lovely manners, he would not strangle the most tiresome of mistresses.

" Anything more to go on? " he encouraged his visitor.

" Oh, yes. That's why I'm here. You see, I know of another man who used to visit Mrs. Foster and, Mr. Crook, he was in Martindale that night."

Crook, whose usual stance resembled a sack of potatoes, sat up hard. " Praise the pigs! " he ejaculated. " A reliable witness at last. Don't know his name, sugar? "

" No. But I should recognise him anywhere. He's a powerfully-built man, with very striking auburn hair . . ."

" Coppernob! " declared Crook. " I knew we'd work him into the picture sooner or later. Well, that makes two of us. Now—regardin' the dear departed. Not a friend of yours, I take it? "

If Stella had not been dead already Addie's glance would have transfixed her. It was compounded of one part contempt and three parts pure hate. For one instant Crook felt as if he had wandered into the Large Snake House.

" She was no one's friend, Mr. Crook," Addie replied with deadly emphasis. " From my first sight of her I knew she was Mr. Henry's enemy."

" How come, sugar? " Play it down, he was thinking. Like Mr. Gradgrind, what he wanted were facts, not facts with so much parsley round the dish you couldn't tell the original nature of its contents. " Start at Chapter One. How long have you known she was your Mr. Henry's cup of cold pizen? "

" A few weeks. That's all." She paused, as if surprised at her own moderation. " It seems as if I must have known much longer than that, but it was one evening when I was coming back from Martindale Hospital. I was visiting there. My friend—the odd thing is that Friend's her name, Amy Olivia Friend, A.O.F. You see? "

" Not yet," confessed Crook handsomely. " Go on talkin' and maybe I'll get there in the end."

" Amy's a nurse so, naturally, she doesn't have to go into one of the public wards at Martindale, which means I can visit her any time, within reason, of course. I used to go over about twice a week. She was in hospital for two months. She has a great many friends, and some of them like myself can only visit in the evening, so we arrange not to overlap. Tuesdays and Fridays were my evenings. One Friday I was coming away down Hallett

Street. It would be—oh, a little after half past seven,
I should think. On Martindale evenings I always stopped
and had a meal at the Clover Café at the far end of
Hallett Street—quite moderate and nice *English* cooking.
I leave the hospital about a quarter to seven—the last
meal in the private rooms is seven o'clock and they like
visitors to be gone a few minutes earlier, though of course
you can visit after dinner, if you like. Only I never did.
I usually had some work to finish off at home. I happened
to glance across the road and to my surprise I saw Mr.
Henry walking along on the other side, coming from the
other direction. He was carrying some flowers, and I
thought he was probably visiting a dependant of one of our
ex-employees. Hallett Street is quite *small* houses, you
see."

Crook saw. The tenants of such houses would not be in
Henry's class range was what she meant.

" Naturally, I pretended I hadn't seen him. I've known
for a great many years that he likes to keep his office
and his personal lives quite separate. But it so happened
that as *I* drew abreast of Number 17 on my side of the
road, he stopped and opened the gate and for some
reason I couldn't help glaning accross, and so I saw
her. She opened the door and I saw her quite clearly."

" Clearly enough to know her next time? "

" Oh, yes. My long sight is quite abnormally good. I
wear spectacles for work, but never out-of-doors. And—
I saw her described in one of the papers as a striking
personality. I don't know about that. I only saw at
once that she was—dangerous. Dangerous to Mr. Henry,
that is."

Her voice told him that she was not concerned with
Stella Foster's effect on anyone else. " I know it's easy to
be wise after the event," she continued earnestly, " but
when I got home I made a note in my diary. I keep rather
a detailed diary, it's—companionable. You don't have
to be on your guard—it's like having a friend you can
always trust . . ."

Crook unexpectedly put out a big hand and covered

hers. " I get you, sugar. You didn't speak of this to anyone else, of course? Not Amy Whatsername, or——? "

" Of course not. I shouldn't dream of discussing Mr. Henry with anyone. But I was worried, Mr. Crook. You see, it was obvious to me that he hadn't the smallest notion that she might be dangerous. He has a most unsuspicious nature, and . . ."

" And he always expects the chips to fall the way he wants them? O.K., sugar, I have hunches, too. Still, what I don't get is why Mrs. Foster should get in your hair."

" Because it was quite, quite obvious that she wasn't a dependant, that is, not anyone to do with the firm. I realised at once that she was . . ." She paused, agonised with embarrassment.

" The Big White Chief's girl-friend. Now, come, sugar, neither you nor me was born yesterday, and there's been girl-friends since the days of Cleopatra."

" Yes. Oh, yes." She clasped her hands with unconscious drama. " But you see, there was Miss Carr."

" Meaning you knew about her? " But, of course, she did. You couldn't hope to keep your secrets from her sort. These Old Girls, they knew everything.

" You mustn't think me prying, Mr. Crook, but one evening when I went in with Mr. Henry's letters, he was writing one by hand, and that was very unusual in itself. He used to make a little joke about it, say his education had been so neglected he couldn't write anything except his signature. He gave me the letter to stamp and I saw it was addressed to Miss Carr. Not that I hadn't guessed before that—I had seen Miss Carr with him once, she's young and very attractive, and of course quite desperately in love."

" You could see that, too? " Crook's big red brows lifted.

" Any woman could have seen it, and any woman who knew Mr. Henry could understand it. So, as I say, I couldn't fit this Mrs. Foster in with Miss Carr. And I was sure she spelt trouble. There was no one I could speak to about it, and it wasn't my concern, but I did wish I could warn him. I did try in a rather roundabout way at the anniversary luncheon—I had to make a speech and I tried to work in a warning he would understand and no one else would, but I'm not very clever at being subtle, and I could see he hadn't understood a word. It was different with Mr. Avery."

"You mean, he did understand?" Crook's voice quickened with excitement.

"On the way back from the Bull he asked me what I was trying to tell him—Mr. Henry, I mean—but I couldn't say much before Mr. Henry joined us, and after that it was too late. Not that Mr. Avery could have done anything, but I did wish there was someone in whom I could confide."

"Here's your chance," said Crook, cordially. "Where does Coppernob come in?"

About four chapters ahead, he supposed, and if possible he would like to skip the intervening three.

"That was about a week later, less than a week, it was the following Tuesday. I was coming down Hallett Street again when I saw a big grey car draw up opposite Number 17 and this man got out. Mrs. Foster must have been expecting him, because she came to the door and they got into the car, and drove away. Mr. Crook, if thoughts could have killed, she would have been dead before she reached her destination, wherever it was. She was playing fast and loose with Mr. Henry, treating him as one of a crowd . . ." Her hands in their dark fabric gloves clenched so that the big knuckle-bones showed stark.

"Take it easy, Boadicea," Crook warned her. "She had the right to go out with a pal. The days of slavery are over."

Miss Bainbridge's next words nearly made him jump out of his skin. "She was a strumpet," said Addie. "I know it's not a pretty word, but it's in the Bible and it's the only word that fits her. I dare say there were others, in fact, I know there were, because, after that, I threw pride to the winds and—and deliberately spied on her.

I went to Martindale nearly every night, whether Amy expected me or not, and I used to walk down Hallett Street. And I saw her several times. Once she was going into a public house, and another time I saw her with quite a different man, and once she was with the one you call Coppernob. Oh, she was quite promiscuous, Mr. Crook. You do appreciate why I felt so anxious on Mr. Henry's behalf? "

"Sure, sure." Crook was soothing. "Now, you're dead certain you saw this party in Martindale on the night Mrs. Foster snuffed it? "

"I'm absolutely certain. I had walked down Hallett Street as usual—it was one of my regular days for visiting Amy in hospital and she was expecting to be discharged the following week—and he was there in the car park, just locking his car."

"The time bein'? "

"About a quarter to eight. I was later than usual because of the rain. I hadn't been prepared. I hurried into the Public Library at the top of the hill. I waited there in the reading-room till it cleared—it was very off-and on that night, if you remember—and then I thought-if I stopped for a meal at the Clover Café I should be late coming down Hallett Street. Besides, it's very popular and most of the best dishes are off by seven-thirty. It closes at eight, so one way and another I hadn't had my evening meal. I went to the Help Yourself place in the High Street, quite good, but not my idea of comfort. I do like to read during a meal, and when you're perched up on a stool, it's not so easy."

"I'll say," said Crook, kindly. Reading was one of the things he was going to take up when he retired, and he did not expect to do that till he was ripe for the church-yard. "By the way, said any of this to the police? "

"Of course not. I haven't worked in a lawyer's office for thirty years without learning that evidence without proof isn't evidence at all. The fact that this man was in Martindale on the night Mrs. Foster was murdered doesn't mean he was with her or was involved. He may have half a dozen friends in Martindale, it may just have been a coincidence."

" Or, of course," suggested Crook, steadily, " it could be it was just a happy inspiration on your part that he was there at all."

Miss Bainbridge didn't take offence; she said in surprised tones, " If I know enough law to realise you can't bring accusations without some kind of foundation, I know enough to understand the folly of false statements. If he wasn't in Martindale, no doubt he can produce witnesses to show where he was."

" Your point," said Crook, grinning. These old girls, you never got the better of them. " Well, Miss Bainbridge, I couldn't have done better myself—keeping your mouth shut and then coming to Henry Greatorex's defence for advice."

Miss Bainbridge stood up, straightening the remarkable hat and smoothing down the fingers of her fabric gloves.

" I can't tell you what a weight you have taken off my mind," she assured him, earnestly. " I feel quite certain I can leave everything to you. And now I must really be going. I came up from Beckfield by the day coach. I have a—a thing about trains. I wonder if I am a railway hoodoo. I have a secret dread every time I travel by rail that there will be an accident, and it wouldn't be only I who might get hurt, but every other soul on board."

" Oh, come," Crook rallied her, " there's plenty of accidents when you ain't travelling."

" That is true, of course, like that shocking affair the other day, the very night Mrs. Foster met her end. I remember reading about it, it made me feel quite queer. I couldn't sleep for thinking of all those ordinary people— a lot of them were day tourists, you know—all making plans for the next morning and remembering what they had to do, count the laundry and send something to the cleaners and order the coal, just the usual things, and then suddenly coming to an end."

She took herself off, still apologising for her " intrusion."

" Know who I wouldn't like to be? " Crook observed

to Bill Parsons when she had gone. " Our Mr. Sumner. She'd strangle him with her own hands if she could, and if it 'ud help Henry Greatorex. And she could, come to that, they're big enough. And though she may lie awake worryin' about the victims of a railway accident, she wouldn't lose a ha'porth of sleep on *his* account."

CHAPTER X

GERALD SUMNER had never met anyone like Arthur Crook before, and when he heard that a man of that name had asked for an interview with an eye to business, he decided he was one of these get-rich-quick johnnies who wanted to spend some of his brass building some monstrosity to be known as Crook's Castle or something equally fatuous. When Crook came bursting in, he decided he'd made a pretty good guess, so that he was nearly knocked off his pins when Crook pitched one of his professional cards on the table and said, " Acting for the defence in the Foster murder. Thought you might be able to give me a bit of help."

Gerald was shocked into immobility for a moment. Then he recovered himself and repeated, " The Foster murder? "

" Not a readin' man? " suggested Crook, amiably. " Look, my time's money and I daresay it's the same with you. Occurred to me that, seein' you knew the lady . . ."

" You're misinformed," interposed Gerald, sharply.

" If so, I'm in good company. Listen. I was in the Nell Gwynn the night she came marching in, lookin' like hell's delight, and I was there when you came marchin' back, havin' deposited your female burden, and took her home. Hold it, hold it, I ain't through yet. You were seen that night, at least your car was, standing in front of the gate of Number 17."

" Who says so? " demanded Gerald.

" The lady opposite. She should know, seeing she spends most of her wakin' hours at the window."

" You really imagine the police would take her evidence —a snooper like that? Why, what she didn't see she'd invent."

" I suppose that's what Mrs. Foster told you? " Crook murmured. " Otherwise, I don't see how you'd know."

" Why have you come to me? " Gerald demanded.

136

" I've told you. I'm acting for the defence. My job is to get my man off the rope. Now, it could be Mrs. Foster confided in you somewhat, told you about the anonymous letter, about being threatened, showed you her little gun . . ."

" I had no idea she had a weapon until I read the report of her death."

" So you had heard? I had wondered how you came to miss it. Now, don't give me that one again about not knowin' her, because I've got another witness, as well as the evidence of my own eyes, and this one is the kind every jury believes, one of those industrious dames that don't have enough to do all day, plus a bit of overtime, but have to sit down every evenin' and write out what's happened since dawn, before they go to sleep."

" A diary, you mean? A very neat idea, Mr.—er—Mr. Crook, but that could be fixed."

" Not if you knew Miss B. Besides, she's been keeping her record quite a while, knew about Henry Greatorex doin' a spot of visiting, too. According to her notes, you were in Martindale on Mrs. Foster's last night on earth."

He was purposely melodramatic, but if he hoped Gerald was going to play ball he was going to be disappointed. His opposite number put back his head and let out a contemptuous roar.

" The poor lady's overplayed her hand there. As it happens, on that evening I was kept late here, dealing with a quotation for a Youth Hostel. I telephoned my wife to tell her I shouldn't be in to dinner. I dare say she might remember."

" So she might," agreed Crook. " Any special reason why she should remember that night more than another?"

" You've just told me yourself. It was the night Mrs. Foster was killed."

" I thought you didn't know Mrs. Foster, so why should you remember the date?"

" We discussed the matter, naturally. We don't get murders every day of the week in the country."

" And you said to Mrs. S., 'Now, isn't that a funny

thing? That's the night I was kept late in London.'"

" I said nothing of the kind. But I happen to remember that night because there was a boxing programme on the television that I particularly wanted to see. If you disbelieve me," he added, with a courtesy as grim as death, " you can confirm it by looking up the programmes for that evening."

" Oh, I'm darned sure there was a boxing programme that night, you wouldn't be fool enough to tell a story that could be so easily disproved. But—it wasn't the night of the Big Fight, was it? "

" No. But there were some very promising youngsters. I've always been interested in boxing ever since I went up to Oxford. I was quite a useful middleweight in my time. So I wanted to see these young fellows. The programme came on about nine or nine-fifteen. I'm not quite certain which. I missed the first few minutes— I caught the 8.2 from London instead of my normal train which is the 6.5 . . ." He faced Crook belligerently. " Satisfied? "

Crook put on his alligator smile. " Well, would you be? I mean, why stay in London late that one night when you specially wanted to see a television programme? "

" It wasn't that one night. I'd been detained on several recent evenings. This is a big commission if my firm can get it. It's important to me."

" And of course, gettin' my client off is important to me. To say nothing of it's bein' important to him. Well, it's been nice knowing you. I dare say we'll be meeting again soon."

" I can assure you I can give you no further assistance. It amazes me that you should suppose I could."

" With complications he can cope, And every morn leaps forth in hope, Remembering Life's a lottery," quoted Crook. " By the way, anyone stay at the office with you? No? That's too bad, ain't it? "

" I don't doubt you would get round that all right," said Gerald savagely. " Suggest I'd suborned a member of my staff . . ."

"You think of everything, don't you? Well, think up something else good for next time. You're goin' to need it."

And off he went.

In the outer office he said casually to the clerk, "Not got a copy of the midday edition, I suppose?"

"We don't have it," said the clerk, looking down his long nose. "Only the late night final. You can get one at the corner," he added.

"I should have come later," said Crook. "Then it 'ud have arrived. Which d'you prefer? *Record* or *Gazette?*"

"We have the *Gazette.* Personally I plump for the *Record.* My wife likes it. But if it's the gees you want . . ."

Crook did not wait for him to finish that. He had established his point, that Sumner had the *Gazette* delivered at his office; and Henry Greatorex had seen a copy of the *Gazette* in Stella Foster's room; and Gerald had insisted that he was in London that night. All that remained now was to break Coppernob's alibi, "and Bob's your uncle," reflected Crook, leaving the architect's office and emerging into the whirling traffic of the Strand. It was all Lombard Street to a china orange that the newsagent put some identifying mark on the papers— either a name or an address—in which case it would be as good as signing a confession to leave the paper in the dead woman's room.

"Wonder who'd remember he wasn't in his office that night?" Crook debated, walking up Kingsway. Somehow or another, Sumner's alibi had to be destroyed.

Mrs. Rose Carlo (she had married an Italian some years before and lost sight of him, without regret, not long afterwards) was a cleaner at Bulstrode House, where Sumner and Pryce had their offices. She came on duty at six o'clock in the evening and worked her way steadily through the first and second floors. A Mrs. Burnett did the ground floor and basement, and a Mrs. Royle undertook the upper floors. Bulstrode House was not a large building and the three women managed the work very well between them. Mrs. Carlo had had this job for some years, and was known to be conscientious and good-tempered. She was also punctual and regular, and if she spent rather more of her earnings at the Blue Rabbit than a moralist might approve, that, as she would have been the first to point out, was her own affair.

" We all have our little luxuries," she would observe. " When I had Carlo I couldn't have my proper nourishment. Now I'm quit of him I can afford to indulge."

She was cleaning away with her usual vigour and thinking of the black velvet she would have at the day's end when she heard steps on the stairs. She took her scrubber out of her pail and frowned. They were a man's steps and they weren't the night watchman; for one thing, he wasn't yet due and for another he did not walk with that buoyant tread. Like a sack of coals falling down a chute, that was Eddie Baynes. Mrs. Carlo was indignant. The floor belonged to her at this hour of the day; she supposed one of the clerks, careless fellow, had forgotten something his wife had told him to bring home. Well, he had best be quick about it and not let her catch sight of him. She had known women who didn't object to overtime on the part of the staff, but she had always stood firm. Once you gave an inch you found you could not brush for the feet in your way. Besides, it was not natural, wanting to work late, and she backed nature all the time.

The door flew open and an apparition appeared on the threshold. Round, spry and brown, like a bun dressed up for the Easter parade, reflected Mrs. Carlo, irreverently.

" Well," she said, sitting back on her heels, " look what's blown in. Father Christmas in mufti. You've got your dates wrong, young fellow."

" Talking to me? " asked Crook, who knew he would never see fifty again.

" That's right. Who are you looking for? "

" You, sugar," said Crook, simply. " You on duty five nights a week? "

" That's right, though what it's got to do with you ..."

" Easy to see no one ever wrote WELCOME on your doormat," Crook riposted. " Anyone here—besides you, I mean? "

" In this office—no. Work stops at five-thirty 'ere. I don't say they mightn't go on another five minutes or so, I wouldn't know, I don't come till six. On the dot, mind you, but they've all got the sense to be out of the way by that time. Never absent, never late, that's me. You can set your watch by me, and anyone 'ull tell you so."

" Does you credit," approved Crook. " Where's the boss? "

" Gone home, of course. Same as always."

" Well, not quite always," Crook demurred. " Puts in a bit of overtime now and again, I hear. And if he likes to work round the clock who's to stop him? "

" Me," said Mrs. Carlo. " Any overtime he does, he does outside this office. I wouldn't have it, I tell you straight. I don't interfere with their working hours, and I don't expect them to interfere with mine."

" Look," said Crook, dangling his brown billycock from a hand not much larger than an ordinary leg-of-mutton, " you're human, ain't you? Though if you were to tell me you were a machine in a Mrs. Mopp apron I'd believe you. Aren't you ever away? get a cold? tummy ache? trouble with the old man? "

" Not me. When I undertake a job I carry it through. And my old man blew away on a gale years ago and good riddance."

Crook transferred his hat to the other hand and offered her the free one.

" Shake. That's my gospel, too. Now, put up your brush for a minute and give me a break. It's a matter of life and death, and I mean life and death."

" Who are you, anyway? " Suspicion clouded her face. " Not the police? "

" You tell them that, and see them laugh the wrong side of their big fat faces. No. What I'm here for is to establish an alibi. Y'see, there's a chap who works here and he says he worked late one Tuesday a few weeks back. Had a big job on hand and couldn't leave it, so, he says . . ."

" I don't care what he says," interrupted Mrs. Carlo, firmly. " And I don't care if he's the boss or the Archangel Gabriel, he never stopped on here on a Tuesday or any other night."

" More than one night," urged Crook.

" Then you've come to the wrong address. It wasn't here. I come at six and I'm here till eight, and I don't go along to the corner for a drop of anything till my work's done. Of course, he might come in later . . ."

" According to him, he catches a train at eight something, so that couldn't be the answer."

" Then it's what I've told you, you've come to the wrong address." She took the scrubber out of the bucket and shook it: drops of soapy water flew out of it. " And if that's not the answer, then it's the other thing."

" Meaning? " Crook insinuated.

" It's a funny thing about men, they never bother to think up a new tale to tell their wives. Kept late at the office, my dear. They must thing we're a soft lot."

" He wouldn't be an easy chap to forget," Crook pursued. " Big chap, copper-plated, bit of a lady's man, I shouldn't wonder."

" I know about these ladies' men, I married one, led me up the garden all right, he did. I've never fancied the country since. And the only Coppernob I've seen in three years is the chap you say good morning to in your shaving mirror every day of the year."

" Good enough," said Crook. " Sorry to have intruded, I'm sure. I'm going across to the Two Doves myself. If you should happen to look in on the way home . . ."

" I don't go for half an hour yet," retorted Mrs. Carlo, sternly. " I was never one to scamp my work and you've gone and wasted a quarter of an hour, as it is."

" What's a little overtime between friends? " grinned Crook. " Well, be seeing you—maybe."

He crossed the street and settled himself cosily in a corner in the bar of the Two Doves. He was pretty sure Mrs. Carlo would be coming along. " Sufferance is the badge of all our tribe," declared Shylock, and curiosity was the badge of Mrs. Carlo's. Sure enough, just after eight o'clock, in she came, accompanied by a stout cheerful friend, the one who had admitted him to Bulstrode House that night. Crook saw them and waved and they came to where he was sitting.

" Take a pew," he offered, " and name your fancy."

When he had brought them their drinks and they were all settled, Mrs. Carlo said, " I was mentioning to my friend here, Mrs. Burnett, the remark you passed about someone being on the premises after six p.m. one Tuesday evening. And she'll bear me out."

" There's one of my gentlemen is inclined to get under my feet a bit," acknowledged Mrs. Burnett, lifting her glass and saying, " Health, I'm sure. But he's a little dark fellow, works late trying to pass an exam. Has family troubles and can't work at home. I must say he don't bother me, and it's not every night, of course. But Mrs. Carlo was saying your gentleman had red hair? " She paused politely.

" That's right," said Crook. He snatched out a pencil and on the back of an envelope produced a caricature of Gerald Sumner that even his wife would have recognised.

Both ladies shook their heads. He didn't ring a bell with either of them, not the teeniest tinkle.

" Have the other half," Crook suggested, going back to the counter. They had earned it, he reflected, putting the kybosh on Sumner's fantastic yarn.

As he set the glasses down on the table Mrs. Burnett leaned forward to say, " I hope this isn't one of them narsty divorce cases? "

" Never touch 'em," said Crook, sincerely.

" Murder now," continued Mrs. Burnett, " that's everyone's business, so to speak, but I don't hold with all this Paul-prying into married life. Nasty-minded, I call it."

" I suppose," offered Mrs. Carlo, wistfully, " it wouldn't be murder."

" Just what it would be," exulted Crook. " Y'see, if X says he was here and he wasn't, and Mrs. X says he wasn't home, and nobody else can tell us where he was— well, it could be he was with the dear departed, helping her to pack up for Kingdom Come," he wound up, with rich anticipation in his voice.

" You mean, one of my gentlemen . . . ? " Illogically, Mrs. Carlo now looked horrified.

" I don't say that." Crook was quick to appreciate a change in the temperature. " Maybe he was taking a blonde out for a quick one, but you know what ladies are."

" Mrs. Burnett and me have both been there before," Mrs. Carlo warned him. " Are you a married man, sir, if I may ask? "

" Need you? " beamed Crook. " Why, there isn't a girl 'ud look at me."

" Not a girl, perhaps," allowed Mrs. Carlo, " but there's many a widow would look twice, and you know what they say—there's many a good tune played on an old fiddle."

Crook said quickly, " Never had any ear for music. Too bad, ain't it? Well, ladies, I'm most grateful . . ."

" You're not going to bring me into court, I hope," said Mrs. Carlo with awful emphasis. " I've kept myself respectable through all my troubles, marriage along of the rest."

" No sense this chap pressing it if I have a witness every juryman will believe to tell them different," promised Crook in his cheerful, ungrammatical way. " Well—if ever I can do anything for you . . ."

But he could see at once neither of them would ever put any business in his way.

Having no previous knowledge of his man, Gerald Sumner had assumed the matter closed so far as he was concerned, and he was startled and secretly apprehensive when he heard that Crook had called for the second time.

He was in two minds as to whether he would see the fellow, but, remembering that pugnacious jaw and resolute handclasp, he changed his mind and said, " I'll see him in ten minutes."

" It's no go, you know," said Crook, barging in ten minutes later, " keeping me hanging about won't change facts. Truth is, I've been testing your alibi and it don't hold water any more than a leaky sponge."

" In that case I wonder you haven't already approached the police."

" I don't want to make myself look more of an ass than I can help," Crook told him with an almost disarming simplicity. " Could be I made a mistake, though I don't believe it myself. You see, I've talked to the lady who cleans your offices and she'll come into court and swear there's never been anyone working late on a Tuesday or any other night for the last month." He eyed the other man thoughtfully. " If you'd been my client," he said, " I'd have warned you against making any statement that could be disproved. And don't tell me a jury wouldn't take her word against yours. Just bear in mind that face that 'ud be more likely to sink a thousand ships than launch 'em."

" I haven't the faintest idea what the cleaner looks like," interpolated Gerald, contemptuously.

" Well, that's funny, seeing you stick to it you were there that night till you caught your train at eight something, and she came on the scenes at six."

" In any case, I should scarcely be likely to recall her appearance."

" You say that because you've never set eyes on her," Crook assured him. " That's what she says and I believe her. And I'll tell you another thing," he added frankly. " If you had been there you'd have scatted before her broom same like the other dust cluttering up the place. It don't surprise me Signor Carlo made himself scarce early on. She probably brushed him off like she would a spider's web. And if you were thinkin' of carryin' on the argument there's the lady on the floor below, Mrs.

Burnett, who'll back up little Carlo through thick and thin. To say nothin' of my other witness who saw you in Martindale that night. Well, put all those together in a bag and shake 'em up, and what do you get? I'll tell you, the benefit of the doubt for my client, and maybe something thrown in for yourself."

" If you imagine you can take this sort of evidence into court . . ."

" Never hear of a sub-poena? And just bear in mind that the police in this country 'ud sooner see the gallows empty than dangle the wrong feller. If I let them know I've got a bit of fresh evidence they'll start nosing round, and they won't be as tactful as me. The sanctity of the home's nothing to the boys in blue."

" If you are proposing to get in touch with my wife," began Gerald in a towering rage, " I can assure you she'll merely confirm my story."

" Wouldn't be much use to us if she didn't," Crook told him. " No court attaches much weight to a wife's evidence. If she backs up her husband, well, that's the natural thing to do; and if she's all for him swinging, they call it malice and unnatural. To hear juries talk," exploded Crook, " you'd think they were none of them married. Fact is, of course, they don't see why they should stand the marriage racket for years and never put the old woman underground, while some bolder chap chances his arm and gets away with it. Now—quite sure you wouldn't care to reconsider your story? "

Gerald looked extremely professional and engaged; he made Crook think of a stuffed whale he had once seen in a museum.

" I can only repeat, I have nothing to add to my previous statement, and as I'm exceedingly busy . . ."

If that last bit was true it was odd that, for a long, long while after Crook's cheerful departure, he sat, head on hand, doing absolutely nothing.

146

CHAPTER XI

GERALD MIGHT have been surprised and perhaps heartened to know that Crook felt as baffled as himself. Avery came marching into 123 Bloomsbury Square to find the lawyer huddled like an enormous brown owl over his desk.

" Am I interrupting? " asked Avery.

" Think nothing of it. As a matter of fact, they say two heads are better than one, and this may prove it. The fact is, Avery, I'm stumped. I'm as good at juggling figures as the next man, but every time I add my two and two it comes to four."

" What," inquired Avery, courteously, " did you want it to come to? "

" Five, of course. The police have already made it four, and if I can't do better than them I'd better have stayed out of the case altogether. What's bothering me," he amplified, " is the time factor. Your uncle says he arrived at Number 17 about eight-thirty. Mrs. Fanshawe she noticed a man swinging in at the gate at about that time, and on the facts we've got it looks as though it should be right. But—it was nine o'clock when Mrs. Shrubsole's pussy tapped at the window to hear the news, and saw Uncle H. haring up the lane. She knows it was nine because of Big Ben and because Pussy's always punctual, and as if that wasn't enough Mrs. Shrubsole's pie-faced husband bears her out. But what the heck was your Uncle Henry doing for half an hour in Mrs. Foster's house unless he was murderin' Mrs. Foster? "

Avery considered. " Shock? " he suggested.

" Lastin' half an hour? Besides, your uncle strikes me as bein' less susceptible to shock than anyone I ever met."

Avery took a chair, and tilted backwards, his hands clasped behind his fair head, his long legs outstretched.

" It's a puzzle," he agreed, mildly.

147

"Your Miss Bainbridge," Crook continued, "is dead sure he didn't do it because he has such lovely manners."

"A very sound piece of deduction," offered Avery.

"That's the way it seemed to me."

He appeared to remember his duties as a host and getting up found some beer in a cupboard and poured out two glasses.

"I've asked him," he continued, "and his only answer is that he stopped being aware of time. Does that make sense to you?"

"Oh, yes," said Avery. "It was like that in the war."

"Your war, perhaps," agreed Crook, grimmer than usual. "In my war time was like the visitor who don't know how to go away. We just sat in those doggone trenches, getting frostbite and pneumonia and watchin' the clock. The hours we wasted—and such uncongenial surroundings. No one can say I'm fussy . . ." He drained his glass at a gulp and refilled it.

Avery tilted his chair forward and began to wander round the room. He stopped in front of a square mahogany-framed mirror and inspected a mark at the corner of his jaw.

"In the wars?" asked Crook, politely.

"Mr. Smith," explained Avery. "A difference of opinion with a boxer. The Scotch are all the same, it's not enough for them to know they're right, everyone else has got to be convinced of it, too. He'd be trying to educate that boxer still if I hadn't intervened."

Crook pushed his second glass of beer aside and stood up.

"I'm gettin' to be an old man, my boy," he confessed sadly. "It's time I applied for some of these National Health spectacles that are going the rounds. Here's a thing been staring me in the face ever since my old girl came to see me, and I never noticed it till now. And if it hadn't been for you starin' at yourself in that glass. Tell me—which side of your face is that mark?"

"The right," said Avery, unmoved.

"Now look in the glass and tell me which side it is."

Avery's fair brows lifted but his voice was unchanged as he replied, " The left, of course."

" Now apply that argument to Miss B's evidence about what she saw in Martindale the night Mrs. Foster was murdered, and see where that gets you."

Avery considered. He took his time about it, but—
" You're like the bedbug," Crook congratulated him. " You get there just the same. Mind you, speculation ain't proof."

" I should have thought, with you, it came to much the same thing," was Avery's casual rejoinder. " All the same, does it help? "

" It could," said Crook. " That's where you can help me with a little experiment. Too cosy if Coppernob's been telling the truth about bein' on the train that got in at nine or thereabouts. Puts quite a new complexion on things, don't it? "

The 8.6 bus from Beckfield to Wolverton was just starting when a tall young man, accompanied by a girl wearing a blue scarf over her dark hair came racing up and jumped aboard.

" Praise the pigs, as Crook would say," remarked Avery, dropping into his seat. " I'd never have dared face him again if we'd missed that."

" There's a later one, isn't there? " Beverley seemed unconcerned.

" From Crook's point of view, there's never more than one of anything."

" Why are we going to Wolverton? "

" To see how long it takes."

" And what do we do when we get there? "

" Come back again."

" On another bus? "

" There isn't another into Beckfield to-night, or rather there won't be, by the time we arrive. No, we're coming back by train—we hope."

" And if we don't? "

" Crook won't like it at all," was Avery's calm reply.

"To hear you speak," exclaimed Beverley, "you'd think Mr. Crook was a sort of major prophet."

"I hope it's true." Avery's voice deepened, soberly. They spoke very little on the journey, each occupied with secret thoughts. When the bus reached Wolverton bus stop, which was just outside the station, Avery leaped up and jumped out. A London train was disgorging its passengers on the farther platform. Avery, with Beverley at his side, swung himself on to one of the coaches. A porter called warningly, "All change. Train stops 'ere," he added, for the young man's benefit. Beverley dropped back on to the platform, Avery paid no heed. He ran through two coaches, one of which was the Pullman dining-car, dropped out of the train at the farther door, and crossed to the local train standing in No. 2 bay. This he caught with about four minutes to spare.

"What did all that mean?" Beverley wanted to know.

"That Crook's hit the jackpot again. I must ring him up from Beckfield. By the way, how are you getting on, dossing down with Addie?"

"We have a lot in common," Beverley assured him. "And so," she added, "have you. She's sold on Mr. Crook, too."

And Beverley and Addie Bainbridge were sold on Henry, the young man reflected. He felt sorry for any judge that dared pronounce the death sentence on old Uncle Handsome. These two devoted women would be capable of lying in wait for him when he left the court and making him the next candidate for the Mortuary Stakes.

When Crook had Avery's report he said, "Well, that changes things a bit, don't it?"

"Where do we go from here?" inquired Avery.

But if he expected Crook to be down-hearted, he didn't know his man. King Bruce, watching the most famous spider in history, had nothing on Crook. Seven times? he would say. Seventy times seven, if need be. So now, in reply to Avery's question, he said with a sort of serene heartiness, " Oh, now I fancy we're all set for the finale. I'll send you an invitation to the last act, and bring your thinking cap with you. You're going to need it."

In almost every quarter to which Crook had directed his invitation, this was received with suspicion. Gerald Sumner burned to refuse, but feared the square-built, unconventional lawyer from London who, he was convinced, wouldn't hesitate to pull his punches; so he accepted on the ground that, when you are being stalked, it is preferable to keep your enemy in view. He considered taking a lawyer along with him—that would cook Crook's goose all right—but on second thoughts he realised that Trevanion would tell him not to be a damned fool and play into this fellow's hands. His situation was sticky enough as it was.

Peter Garland was startled, and no better pleased than Sumner. He had met Crook on one previous occasion, immediately after that human dynamite had accepted the defence of Henry Greatorex.

" Just checking over your statement," Crook assured him, blandly, when he had run him to earth in a rather seedy hotel. " I mean, there might be something you wouldn't want the police to know that you'd confide in a brother sinner."

Garland had stiffened like an animal scenting danger. There was quite a lot concerning Mrs. Foster that he wouldn't want his wife or anyone else to know, and he doubted if Crook had ever heard of a whisper. The sort of fellow who went about preceded by a brass band, he reflected, uncharitably. He thought of Mrs. Garland, that pale, inscrutable woman who probably saw so much more than she ever let on. He was not afraid of a divorce action, Minnie came of staunch nonconformist folk who disapproved of broken marriages, but he was devoted to his little girl; the thought of being separated from her brought him out in a cold sweat. He had told Crook pretty sharply that he had nothing to add.

"Can't blame me for nosing round, can you?" Crook had inquired.

Garland moved uneasily. The last thing he wanted was Crook nosing about among his affairs. When he got Crook's invitation to a round-table conference at an inn called the Blue Boar at nine p.m.—an hour, suggested Crook, that should suit everyone's convenience—his first impulse was to refuse, but then, like Gerald, he realised that in his own interests he must be present.

Miss Bainbridge experienced no such hesitation. She assured Crook that all she wanted was to see Henry cleared, and was at his disposal at any time. And in a very plain dark felt hat, as stark as a man's derby, and an equally plain dark coat, she arrived at precisely the hour quoted.

Mrs. Fanshawe was frankly delighted to be included in the party. Her sister, still with them and looking, thought Joe, alarmed, as though she were taking root, was stiff with resentment at being ignored.

"I was there that night same as you," she exclaimed. "He's got no right to leave me out."

"Chap's earned a medal asking either of you," observed Joe with unwonted courage. "If he'd asked the pair he'd be fit for a straight-waistcoat."

Avery would come, of course, though Crook hadn't anticipated that Beverley Carr would insist on accompanying him.

"Anything that concerns Henry concerns me," she said.

"Now, look, sugar." This was Crook at his most persuasive—"There's nothin' you can give us, because you weren't even in the country when the poor lady handed in her dinner-pail."

"Except faith in Henry," Beverley insisted.

Crook's round brown eyes flew wider than before. "He's got me," he pointed out.

"It's not the same thing. Mr. Crook, I must be there. You know the old saying about the looker-on seeing most of the game. I can watch, as it were, from the edge."

"As full of prejudice as an egg's full of meat," was

Crook's grim comment, but he knew that if he locked his door against her she'd come sliding down the chimney or pop up through a trap-door like Nellie Wallace in the pantomimes of his boyhood.

He didn't mention to any of them his surprise witness, so when they assembled, all on the dot, that Friday evening, no one recognised the rather pale and sober couple who were there when they arrived.

"Meet Mr. and Mrs. Shrubsole," offered Crook. "Mrs. Shrubsole's goin' to be one of our star witnesses."

Mr. Shrubsole, a square-built man stamped with the marks of the Civil Service, feeling like a sedate riding hack who's suddenly found himself pulled into a circus, glared about him. He had not wanted to accept the invitation, either.

"I know these lawyers," he told his wife. "Twist facts into any shape that suits them. You can't tell them anything, and he's no right to try and put the responsibility on to you. All you saw was a chap going down the lane, for a fraction of a minute, on a dark drizzly night. Does he suppose you could recognise the fellow again, even if he was put on a platform with the spotlight playing on him? Of course you couldn't."

"He doesn't think Mr. Greatorex is guilty, Bruce," insisted his wife. "If anything I say can save an innocent man from the gallows . . ."

"We don't know that he is innocent. Most likely he isn't. And I object to this fellow, Crook, dragging you into the affair. He's got your statement and you've nothing to add."

"Then what are you afraid of?" asked Laura Shrubsole, simply.

"I don't want to find reporters on my doorstep, asking questions and printing answers you won't recognise. I wish you wouldn't go, Laura."

But Mrs. Shrubsole said it would not make any difference, if Crook meant to have her at the gathering he would be capable of hovering over the house in a helicopter till she gave in. So Mr. Shrubsole said in that case he would come, too, making it perfectly clear to Crook that neither of them could be of any assistance to him whatsoever.

"That's what you think," Crook told him blithely. And indeed neither the Civil Servant nor his wife had the smallest idea of the shock Crook had in store for them.

So there they were—Sumner and Garland, Stella's one-time admirers, Addie Bainbridge who had hated her, Mrs. Fanshawe, the sensationalist enjoying it up to the hilt, and who had hated her, too, Avery, tall and pale and too dispassionate to be true, Beverley, sheet-white but resolved, the Shrubsoles sitting a little apart from everyone else, and Crook as ruthless as the H-bomb, dominating them all.

Along one wall of the room was one of those great mirrors with gilt edges, reflecting half the room, and Crook had cunningly disposed the chairs to give him a view of the expressions and movements of all those present, without appearing to be on guard. He opened the proceedings as tersely as the snap of a rifle.

"I don't want to keep anyone longer than I need," he said, "and I'll start by sayin' two things. The first is, that I don't think this was a premeditated crime. I don't believe anyone went to Number 17 that Tuesday night on murder bent. Come to that, I'm not even sure this is murder. Murder has to have malice aforethought, and my own view is that X didn't see red till Mrs. Foster produced her little gun, and maybe waved it about a shade too freely. Y'see, where there's murder there has to be a motive, unless you're dealin' with madmen, which here I take it we ain't, and who had one? You," he butted his great red head in Gerald's direction, "were crazy about her, you," indicating Peter Garland, "thought of her as a nice piece of homework. . . ."

"And in any case didn't get inside the house that night," the young man pointed out, mildly.

"Can't blame me for trying to show you did, not if it helps my client," was Crook's spirited reply. The young man turned pale. This was just what he had feared.

Little things like proof didn't bother Crook; it would not worry him if everyone present, saving perhaps the girl and Avery Greatorex, strung themselves on a row of lamp-posts, if it helped his precious client. He did not even care about establishing the truth, he just wanted to get his man off the rope, and it was nothing to him who paid the piper.

"Mrs. Fanshawe and Mrs. Shrubsole, and it's very public-spirited of them to come to-night at all, are here to give evidence for the defence," Crook continued, adding heartily, " and if they don't know it now they soon will. Avery here is holding the book for the family, and the young lady's his guest. Miss Bainbridge—well, we'll come to her pretty soon. You could say it's thanks to her we're holding this meeting at all. Now, let's start with the second thing I referred to a while back. We're faced with a time-table and a set of facts, and it'll be obvious to everybody they can't all be true, and our job to-night is to sort the wheat and the chaff.

" According to the doctor, death must have taken place between six and ten p.m., he won't be more definite than that, and you can't blame him, seeing she wasn't found till the next day. So—here's the time-table, and let's see what we can make of it.

" Six o'clock—the earliest time she could have been killed—she was seen by Mrs. Fanshawe and her sister on their way out to the cinema. O.K.? "

" That's right," said Mrs. Fanshawe, eagerly.

" Six-twenty. Mr. Garland sets out for Martindale. Right? "

" More or less," acknowledged Peter, cautiously. Crook was like Mark Twain's famous jumping frog—you never knew where his next leap would take him.

" There was a call for you at six-thirty and you'd gone. All the times could be cut five minutes either way, I don't doubt," conceded Crook generously. " Seven-ten (say) Miss Hunter sees Mr. Sumner alightin' at Pheasant Green. Yes, I've seen her and got her story, too. O.K. O.K.," as Gerald was about to burst into indignant speech, " I told you they couldn't all be true. About the same time my client arrives at Martindale Hospital, Miss Bainbridge having left about a quarter of an hour earlier. They didn't meet. Right? " His brown eyes rolled in Addie's direction.

" That is correct, Mr. Crook."

" Next thing we hear of Miss Bainbridge seein' Mr. Sumner with his car in the car park. According to him he's still in London, but we'll deal with that presently. Eight o'clock my client leaves the hospital—vouched for by a doctor and the matron, who met the doctor on arrival—and Mr. Garland here starts asking at the Horn of Plenty for Mrs. Foster. Eight-thirty Mr. Greatorex arrives at Number 17 and is seen by Mrs. Fanshawe—that is, we're assuming the man she saw was my client, and I defy the whole bench of Law Lords to prove anything different. At—eight thirty-five, was it? " he looked inquiringly at Addie, " you caught your home-going bus."

" They run every hour from Martindale at thirty-five minutes past the hour," elaborated Miss Bainbridge.

" Mr. Garland's moved on to the Coach and Horses by this time, but Mrs. F. ain't there either. Now, by eight-thirty, according to my client, and naturally it's his version I'm going to take into court, Mrs. Foster is already dead. Mr. Sumner says he can't be responsible because he didn't leave London till after eight. Mr. Garland tried the house at nine o'clock or thereabouts and couldn't get in. But Miss Bainbridge sticks to her story of seeing Mr. Sumner at seven-fifty. And as if that wasn't enough, we have Mrs. Shrubsole with her story of a dark figure in the lane as Big Ben struck the hour. If we can identify that figure, we know who put out Mrs. Foster's light. The police say it was Henry Greatorex, and he don't deny being in the neighbourhood at the time. Miss Bainbridge had caught her bus and Mr. Sumner's train was just drawing into Pheasant Green and he was recognised by an official on the platform. I've tried and tried but I don't see any way of shaking that. So, seeing my client's got to be innocent, it seemed to me that if we got together and pooled the facts, we might find an opening."

He glanced casually in the mirror. One of the reflections he saw there belonged to a murderer and Murder knew it. So that was how the wind was blowing, Murder warned Murder's other self. You might have known the chap had something up his sleeve besides his arm, but —what had he discovered, what discrepancy had caught that tireless round brown eye, and—could he prove it? That was the point to recall. Speculation, no matter how accurate, got you nowhere, you had to have proof. *And of proof there was none.* Still, keep your head, admit nothing, volunteer nothing, there are witnesses all round you to any piece of folly you may commit. Anything you say may be taken down and used in evidence, used in evidence, used ... The man's eyes were hooded now like a crow about to pierce its cruel beak into its victim ... a silly comparison, really, since a crow that looked anything like Crook would be in the Natural History Museum. And whatever he suspected he could prove nothing, though he would be prepared to pin the crime on Mrs. Shrubsole's kitty sooner than see his man go into the witness-box to be cross-examined on a charge of murder. So—keep your eyes down, your hands folded under the edge of the table where no one can see them, don't volunteer information, remember silence is golden, silence is golden.

" Well, now," Crook continued cheerfully, " we've got all these statements and some of 'em, to put it mildly, conflict, so let's see what we can make of them. Mr. Sumner's our chief puzzle. He seems to have been popping about like a flea in a gale of wind that night. Miss Hunter sees him at Pheasant Green at seven-five, Miss Bainbridge sees him at Martindale at seven-fifty, the ticket collector sees him at Pheasant Green at nine-six, or whatever it was, and Mrs. Sumner sees him come in at nine-fifteen. So—how come? "

" All those statements can't be true," declared Miss Bainbridge flatly.

" That's where you're wrong, sugar," rebuked Crook. " They could be, and it's my belief they are. Only— you're a woman and the ladies will jump to conclusions." He gave her his famous baby alligator grin to take the sting out of the words. " You saw Mr. Sumner in the car park, maybe with the car keys in his hand, so you decided he'd just arrived. But *suppose you were wrong? Suppose he was unlocking the car to take her back to Pheasant Green?* "

" Why on earth . . . ? " began Sumner, but " Pipe down," Crook told him pleasantly. " I'm coming to that. You had to be seen arriving at the time you said on the telephone to Mrs. S., and if someone could notice your arrival, so much the better. And I will hand it to you, Sumner, you can think fast, and in your line and mine thinkin' fast is sometimes as useful as bein' quick on the draw. You hadn't forgotten, had you, that passengers on the eight-two from London have to change at Wolverton and get a diesel train from the bay? Now say you could pick up that train, who's to say you didn't come right the way from town just like you said? And it could be done. Oh, yes, it could. Young Avery here tried it out the other night. What you do is park your car round the corner at Pheasant Green, pick up a local bus to Wolverton— it's a nasty, drizzly night, nobody's likely to pick you out among the rest—and when you get to Wolverton you board the London train and collect that little dinner bill you were so proud of."

" Very ingenious," admitted Gerald, " but—merely a conjuring trick. You've no proof, you can't have."

" That's what you think. The trouble with you single-minded chaps is you can only think of one thing at once. All you were thinking of was to give yourself an alibi by having a dinner bill to show. How often in the past has Mrs. S asked to see your dinner bills? Never? Just what I thought. It's being too careful that fits out more men with a rope necktie than any amount of *laissez-faire*. It's like the chap stalking the rabbit and not realisin' the bull's stalking him. You never thought a steward might be a bit curious to see a man sprint along the platform and jump aboard and hustle down to the dining-car. The normal thing if you'd lost something was to look for a porter or somebody and get him to come along, but, of course, you couldn't afford to be seen."

" Why not? " put in Avery, dryly. " He only had to say he'd lost a pencil or something of that kind during dinner, and who was to know he'd just come aboard the train? "

" You're the chap for my money," said Crook, heartily. " You think of everything. Any time you're in trouble you come right along to me and I'll treat you free, gratis and for nothing."

" I dare say if Crook's preposterous story were true I might have thought of asking for a porter, but it's all nonsense. In any case, the train was in a siding, all the lights were out and all the staff had departed. So . . ." He stopped, because Crook was staring at him.

" I'll say it was," he ejaculated, " but how the heck did you know? "

" Because I was there. I left the train at Wolverton with all the other passengers and caught the diesel in Number 2 Bay. The main train was immediately put on a siding. I found myself in a carriage with a chap I sometimes see going up in the morning. We got into conversation. He was complaining about the dinner, the price charged for what he called an inferior meal."

Crook slapped a mighty hand on his thigh as though he were trying to slaughter an outsize gnat.

" So that's how it was done. He produced his meal-ticket to show you the price, you took it, careless like, seeing the chance it provided—of course, you didn't board the other train, *because you never thought of it.* He asked you if you'd dined on board, didn't he, and what you thought? Of course he did, and you'd have to say No, because— you travel on a first-class season, I take it? Well, there's one first-class dining-car on that train, so if you'd been in it, he couldn't have missed you, particularly if you were acquaintances. I suppose you wouldn't care to give me his name? No matter, I can find out, I have my own methods."

" And no holds barred? " sneered Gerald.

Crook's face was suddenly locked as a grille. " My client's likely to swing for murder," he said. " That's crime with a capital C."

" And you want to put me in his place? "

" I don't care who I put in his place. I don't care if nobody swings for the late Mrs. Foster. All that matters to me is that my client don't. You're doin' yourself a lot of harm being so stubborn," he went on, seriously. " If only you could see that by admitting you came back on the bus from Martindale you were franking yourself, you wouldn't be so cagey. Because, if you were aboard that train—and if you'd had as much sense as 'ud go under a pre-war threepenny bit you'd have mentioned this pal of yours before—then it couldn't have been you Mrs. Shrubsole saw sneakin' down the back lane at nine o'clock."

" Of course it wasn't me. It was Henry Greatorex. I understood he'd admitted as much."

Crook leaned back, jingling his old-fashioned watch chain. " Oh, no," he said. " He was comin' *up* the lane. Mrs. Shrubsole's visitor was goin' *down*—down in the direction of Number 17. Ain't that so, Mrs. Shrubsole? "

Shrubsole was about to speak, but his wife put her hand on his knee.

" It's all right, Bruce. Yes, of course he was going down. I remember wondering if he expected to meet someone on such a night."

" Of course you wondered," agreed Crook, heartily. " Why any dame should risk ruining her permanent hanging around a wet gate when she might be necking cosily in the pictures or holding hands at a snack bar beats me, too. Well, then, Sumner, it couldn't have been you. Only—you came into Martindale that night for some reason, and it's all Lombard Street to a china orange it was to see Mrs. Foster. I mean, Miss Hunter's your sister-in-law. It ain't likely she'd be mistaken. And she told your wife and your abigail, who's Conscience Incarnate, that she saw you beetling off in the Bentley in the direction of Martindale. At least you must have taken that turning unless you shot up into the air or went underground, and neither of them seems likely. Then there's Miss Bainbridge's evidence, that you were in the car park at, say, seven-fifty. It wouldn't take you forty minutes to get there from Pheasant Green—so, where were you between, say, seven twenty-five and seven forty-five? Nobody 'ull need more than one guess to answer that one—you were at Number 17. We know the lady was expectin' someone, we know it wasn't Garland here, because she hadn't had his card, we know it wasn't my client because she couldn't be sure when he'd collect his letter from Hive Street, it could have been someone else, but it's asking too much of coincidence to suppose there was another fellow in the picture that night. Besides, you were in Martindale, and you had taken the trouble to ring up your wife and say you were spendin' the evening in London. So if you weren't visiting Mrs. Foster, who were you visiting, and why haven't you produced this person as an alibi? But, of course it was Mrs. F. You wouldn't go visiting anyone else at seven-thirty and be away before eight. Only—after you got there something happened that sent you back to the car park p.d.q. Either you murdered her in the interval, and if you had I take off my hat to you, it's pretty smart work, or else you found someone else had murdered her, and, like a sensible fellow, decided to fade out."

Gerald Sumner threw back his copper-coloured head. "You know all the answers, don't you?" he demanded, savagely. "But I can assure you that Mrs. Foster was alive when I . . ."

"Left the house?" finished Crook, suavely. "Or reached the car park? As to the last, you can't be sure, so you must mean when you left the house. And seeing she was murdered during the next hour, the odds are you could tell us something about the murderer."

" I can tell you nothing," cried Gerald in desperation. " I didn't see Mrs. Foster that night."

" If that's so," said Crook, slowly, " there's only one likely answer, and that is she didn't let you in. If she didn't let you in, it might be because she couldn't, which 'ud suggest that she was dead already, but you're almighty sure she was alive. So—if you didn't see her, you must have heard her. And unless she was like one of these lady novelists that go round talking to themselves, she was talking to someone else. Which means that someone sprang your claim and got in first. Q.E.D. Well? "

Sumner leaned back with the extreme care of a man who is afraid that any spontaneous action will result in breaking something valuable.

" Yes," he said at last. " She had someone with her."

" Well, we've taken long enough to get that far. No idea who it was, of course? "

" None."

" No clues left in the hall? Fancy scarf or . . . ? "

" I didn't see anything."

" But you did get as far as the hall? Yes, of course you did, you've just admitted as much. But tell me this— who let you in? Or did you have a key? "

" No. The door was on the latch."

Crook's big red brows shot up. " That's the tale my client tells. He thought she'd left it for him. Maybe you thought the same? "

" Yes," admitted Gerald, reluctantly. " I thought the same."

" So? '

" I went in. And almost at once I realised she wasn't alone."

" Because," contributed Crook, intelligently, " you heard voices? "

" I heard voices. They were pretty loud voices, because the radio was playing, she always kept it on, and they had to talk above it. At least she did. I didn't hear him say much, to tell you the truth, he didn't have much opportunity. I did hear ' Stella ' once or twice . . ."

" And maybe you heard her call him Peter or Willie or John? " suggested Crook, hopefully.

" No-no. No, I'm afraid I didn't."

" If you were thinking of me," put in Garland, hotly, " you've already got evidence that I wasn't there that night."

" There's other Peters in the world, ain't there? Don't be so touchy." But, come to that, they were all suffering from the jitters and, really, thought Crook, you couldn't blame them. Not that that softened his heart towards one of them. He was as pitiless as a coyote hunting meat for her young. He nodded to Sumner. " Carry on," he said. " We're all attention."

Murder sat listening with the rest, remembering that Cain had borne a brand in his forehead to mark him out from innocent men, and thinking that the human race has made some progress down the ages, since brands are no longer worn. Only—could you be certain that Crook's ruthless eyes didn't discern the brand that was invisible to everyone else?

" I could hear a few phrases from her," continued Sumner in painful tones. " There was no doubt about it, she was in a towering rage, but not a terrified rage, if you understand. I don't know what you think you're doing bursting in here without an invitation . . . something like that. And something about being hard up or not being so hard up—it was all so confused . . ."

" I'll bet it was," agreed Crook. " It didn't occur to you as a good citizen that it might be your job to stop and prevent a murder?"

" I'd no reason to suppose murder was on the cards," protested Sumner in low tones that were more telling than any indignation. " I thought it was a case of double-crossing and suddenly—she didn't seem the woman I had come to meet. To tell you the truth . . ."

" Well, let's have it," encouraged Crook. " It 'ud make a nice change. But you don't have to tell me. I turn'd a cat-in-the-pan once more, And so became a Whig, sir. Meaning the scales fell from your eyes and you saw you were getting yourself tangled up with a proper Kilkenny cat. You have my sympathy, Sumner, honest you have."

And perhaps, if a stone image can look sympathetic, he had.

"I heard one bit more that I recall," continued Sumner in the same jerky agonised voice. "Something about what's it to do with you who I have to visit me? Won't anyone look at you or something of the kind."

"Any answers?" asked Crook.

"No words that I could distinguish. I don't think Stella—Mrs. Foster—gave him much chance—except that I did think I caught the word money."

"Blackmail?" Crook cocked an inquiring red brow.

"I didn't hear enough—I wasn't there more than a minute, you know."

"I know. I know, too, how the dames can be when their dander's up. 'Ammer, 'ammer, 'ammer on the 'ard 'igh road. Bit of a shock to you, I take it?"

"I told you, Mr. Crook, it didn't seem possible this was the same woman. This—this termagant—didn't seem to have any connection with the Stella Foster who—it's no good trying to conceal facts any longer—who infatuated me that night at the Nell Gwynn." He looked straight across at Crook, speaking to him as though they were alone together. "You were there, too. You saw how it was. Didn't you say yourself she was a witch? Well, she bewitched me all right. What's more, I've seen her have precisely the same effect on chaps who'd never set eyes on her before." He looked at Peter Garland. "You know what I mean. You must have seen it at that pub where you met her."

Young Garland nodded. Miss Bainbridge drew a sharp breath as if the situation had become intolerable. Beverley watched her, without speaking. So this, both women were reflecting, was how Henry had once felt, as though the whole world had emptied leaving no one but yourself and Stella.

164

" The macabre thing was," added Gerald, " they'd moved on to a variety repeat on the radio, there was a team of comics on and roars of laughter came thundering through the room, and there was Stella going on and on —I felt a bit light-headed."

" Didn't suspicion that she'd brought out the little gun? " suggested Crook.

" I never even knew she had one."

Crook glanced significantly at Garland, who shook his head.

" I didn't know either."

" I can believe that," Crook acknowledged. " Might be uncomfortable taking tea with a lady who suddenly peppered you with bullets if you spoke out of turn. Still, we do know the gun was produced some time during the evening. I take it you just walked out on the pair," he added to Gerald.

The big man nodded. " I'd begun to suspect a frame-up. In any case, it didn't suit my book to walk in on a scene, tell this chap to get out, and then find I was being had for a sucker. Mind you, Stella knew I was married, and Muriel—my wife—wouldn't have given me a divorce, even if I'd wanted one—which I didn't. The rest of the story is the way you told it. This lady," he glared at Addie Bainbridge, " saw me unlocking my car preparing to get back and try—and try——"

" To save your bacon. What time did you get to the house? "

" She was expecting me at seven-thirty."

" And you were on time? "

Gerald nodded.

" I thought you said you were only in the hall for a minute and the car park's only five minutes from the house, so where were you the rest of the time? "

" I dropped into the Roebuck—it's a quiet little hotel on the corner—I felt I needed something, and it was while I was there I got the idea of going back to Wolverton to see if I could get the connection."

" That's what I don't understand," said Crook. " If

you didn't know there was going to be an inquiry, why be so cagey? "

" I'd told my wife I was coming down on the late train. It occurred to me she might see one of our acquaintances the next day and make some remark—anyway, I couldn't go straight back, it would be obvious I'd been somewhere else, and I didn't feel like making any explanations."

" I'll say," agreed Crook, with emphasis. " You know what they say about the little things. If you hadn't stopped for the drink, Miss Bainbridge wouldn't have set eyes on you and you'd have been in the clear. Now, there's one more point that maybe you hadn't thought of. You didn't set eyes on the visitor and there wasn't any trace in the hall." He leaned forward. " Are you dead sure it was a man with Mrs. Foster that night? "

If he had exploded a grenade in their midst he could scarcely have startled them more. Murder jumped, but reflected that everyone else had done the same. And anyway, Sumner had sworn he had seen nothing. Now, wait for it, wait for it. It was easy to see through Crook's game. He was going to get Sumner going round and round in his mind like a dormouse on its wheel, compelling him to recall some detail that would pinpoint a solution. Sumner looked as dumbfounded as the rest.

" I never thought . . ."

" Think now. Women like Miss F. often make trouble with their own sex. F'r instance, I daresay your wife wouldn't feel exactly matey towards her. No, I'm not trying to drag Mrs. S. in. I know she was sitting at home, with at least two witnesses to alibi her. But there must have been other women. Mrs. Fanshawe here didn't think of her as a sister, and there'd be wives—not yours," he nodded reassuringly to Peter Garland—" we know she's in Wales."

Mrs. Fanshawe interrupted indignantly, " There's a difference between not feeling like a sister and strangling a person," she said.

" Depends on how deep your not liking goes. I've known murder depend on half a dozen ill-chosen words

166

—and I've said all along this murder wasn't premeditated."

"All the same," persisted Mrs. Fanshawe, "you're wrong if you think Mrs. Foster would have invited a woman into her house—specially at that hour of the night."

"That's the point, honey," insisted Crook. "X was there without an invitation. Mr. Sumner here didn't hear much, but he heard enough to realise that. Well, Sumner?"

"I don't know," said Gerald. "It never even went through my mind—like Mrs. Fanshawe, it wouldn't occur to me that Stella would have another woman there. But —I suppose it would be possible. Some women have deep voices, some men have light ones. And I suppose different women react differently. Nothing would have induced my wife to cross her threshold, but other men's wives might not feel the same."

"It don't have to be a wife," said Crook. "And there could be something in what you said about a frame-up. Say Mrs. Foster cultivated you for something more than the pleasure of your society? Rich man, ain't you? She had a little house, rent paid for by someone else, who was backing out. She had a little business, I know, but I dare say she didn't much fancy the notion of having to rely on that. Comfort's like a pussy-cat. You don't notice it much till it's gone. Then you find the house has sort of a cold feel. Mrs. F. may have added you up wrong. She knew you were coming, she left the door of the latch, which was odd in itself, maybe she thinks, when you hear fireworks, you'll come barging in in her defence. Women, you know, they never learn."

"No," said Gerald. "I don't think it was like that."

"To be candid," Crook agreed, "I don't either. And, as I said, it don't even have to be a wife. There's other women besides wives take an interest in a chap's welfare. How about it, sugar?" He turned like a flash to Miss Bainbridge. "*You* knew he visited at Number 17, you knew his present interest lay in another quarter, you're a woman yourself, so you had the dear departed's measure.

You told me so. Me, I don't get to know a dame just by seeing her open a door across the street, but we know the ladies have something called feminine intuition which takes the place of logic. You knew Mr. Sumner was visiting in the same quarter, though I don't say you knew he was going to be there that night, but you were at Martindale, and the times fit like a pair of scissors."

Addie drew a deep, shocked breath. Her big hands in their fabric gloves twisted under the table edge.

" I was visiting my friend at the hospital," she said. " I told you."

" Quite so. But you left the hospital before seven when your friend had her dinner. You didn't go to the Clover Café that night as usual, but you went to a snack bar at the farther end of Hallett Street. You were in the street at seven forty-five, because you walked down past the car park and saw Mr. Sumner there at seven-fifty. So—where were you between seven-ten, say, and seven forty-five? "

" I went into the Public Library, I remember quite distinctly telling you. It stays open till eight. It had turned into a nasty wet evening and I had no umbrella. I didn't want to get wet, colds are such tiresome things, and I was in no particular hurry. I had nothing to do at home."

" Maybe you asked for a book or something, and signed the record? " Crook looked like the monster who welcomes little fishes in with gently-smiling jaws.

" No. No. I just went to the Reading Room."

" And that's where you saw the paper? "

" The paper? " Her face was a greyish colour, her mouth shook.

" Remember telling me how shocked you were about the railway accident? It bothered you all the way home. But *that was only in the evening papers*."

" Yes. I remember now. I bought an evening paper outside the hospital. I thought it would be something to look at during my meal. And then the rain started, and I went into the library. I remember quite well, because the man said it was the last copy he had. He made a little joke about it. Ten thousand a year—being the last, you see," she wound up, desperately.

" Not got it still, by any chance? " But he knew the answer to that one.

" I—I must have left it in the snack bar. I'd read as much of it as interested me, and when you haven't much space papers do clutter up a room so."

" I'm not surprised my client calls you his right hand," Crook congratulated her. " You don't only think of everything, you think of it just when it's wanted."

Avery leaned forward. " Miss Bainbridge, don't let him stampede you. He's no right to question you unless you're willing to reply."

Crook shot the young man a glance of pure poison. " Whose side are you on? " he demanded.

" I'm a lawyer, too," Avery reminded him.

This brief interchange had given Addie an opportunity to collect herself.

" Thank you, Mr. Avery," she said, " but I have nothing to hide. I didn't call on Mrs. Foster. I have never been inside her house."

" Someone was there that night," Crook insisted. " The police say it was Mr. Henry. I'm trying to show it wasn't. Maybe you're shacking up with the police now—a bit late in the day."

" You have no right to say such a thing," cried Miss Bainbridge, and in her agitation her voice sounded as deep as a bloodhound's. " My only interest in this affair has been to establish Mr. Henry's innocence. My only thought for years has been to further his interests." She stared defiantly round her.

" Oh, I believe you," said Crook. " Point is, would you assist him to the extent of puttin' out Mrs. Foster's light if it threatened to burn his house down? The conversation fits, you know. Who asked you to come here? What's it to you who I have in my house? This is where you come in," he continued, turning to Mrs. Shrubsole who had sat goggle-eyed during the past quarter of an hour. " You say you saw someone going down the lane at nine o'clock. We know it wasn't Mr. Sumner, because he was just drawing into Pheasant Green, and it wasn't my client because he was coming *up* the lane. And we know something else. It wasn't someone keeping a date, because no one not fit to be tied would be hanging about on such an evening. No, it was a murderer come to remove a clue—to wit, one copy of the evening paper. Now, I put it to you, Mrs. Shrubsole, a lady in a gentlemanly titfer and a dark coat might look sufficiently like a chap for you not to notice the difference? "

Mr. Shrubsole tried to speak; he was gagged instantly by his wife on one side and Mr. Crook on the other.

" Well, it might," agreed Mrs. Shrubsole, her eyes fixed on Miss Bainbridge. " Mind you, I couldn't go into court and say Yes one way or the other, any more than I could identify anyone, even if the murderer was among the people put up."

Crook beamed. " That's just fine, that's what I hoped you'd say. You're going to be asked to say you saw Henry Greatorex that night. Well, you didn't, and you're going into the box to give evidence for us, never mind which side sub-poenas you."

Mrs. Fanshawe, aching with pity for Lu missing all this good clean fun, broke in to say, " I call it wicked, really I do, to try and hang anyone for the death of a woman like that. In any proper civilisation whoever did it would be called a public benefactor." She leaned across and patted Addie on the knee. " Don't take on, dear," she said. " She was threatening you with the little gun, wasn't she? And everyone has a right to protect themselves."

" Ah, yes," said Crook. " The gun. What made her bring that out? "

" I don't know," said Addie, faintly. " I wasn't there."

" When you heard Mr. Sumner walk into the hall why didn't you sing out? " Crook continued. " Or were you afraid of compromising Mr. Henry? Come to that, maybe you thought it was Mr. Henry."

" As if I wouldn't know Mr. Henry's step," cried Addie, scornfully.

Crook looked up slyly. " I thought you weren't there."

" I wasn't. But if I had been and Mr. Henry had come in I wouldn't have had to wonder who it was. That's all I meant."

" What I'm wondering," continued Crook unmoved, " is what was so important about the newspaper that you —or anyone—'ud risk coming back to the house to collect it. I could understand if it was you," and once more he directed his gaze in Sumner's direction, " because your papers are delivered and they could be traced through the newsagent, but a paper you buy on a street corner and look at in the library, how could that be traced? Why, anyone might think the lady had brought it in herself."

" I told you," said Addie steadily, " I left mine in the snack bar."

" So you did. Well, anyone then." His pitiless brown eyes raked the assembly. " But, of course, it wasn't the paper, was it? It was something that was hidden under the paper, something X forgot in the hurry and peril of the moment. What was it, Miss Bainbridge? A pair of gloves, maybe. You'd take off your gloves when you went into someone's house on a social visit. Sumner says there was nothing in the hall, so most likely you'd put them down in her room, on a chair, and then drop the paper on top of them. And then you go on and have a snack and get ready for the bus and realise the gloves ain't there. You think back—the library perhaps. But no. A lady like you wouldn't walk through the streets without wearing her gloves. So—it has to be the house in Hallett Street. And when Stella Foster's body is found there mustn't be anything there to link you with the death. Eh? Right? " His voice sharpened.

Miss Bainbridge watched him, fascinated, appalled. " They didn't find anything," she said at last, and her voice was almost a croak.

" Sure they didn't find anything, because—you didn't

catch that eight thirty-five bus, did you? You went back up Hallett Street, but you couldn't go in because someone was there already. You had to wait till the coast was clear, get in the back way. Don't tell me you didn't know there was a back way, you'd been going up and down Hallett Street quite a lot these last weeks, and you're an observant dame, you know all the answers. But there's one thing you forgot."

"I don't understand." The words were no more than a shiver of sound.

"Guns make a lot of noise. Mrs. Foster was expecting a boy-friend. When the front-door bell rang that night she never guessed it was Murder coming to call. And a person who's used to making snappy come-backs and not used to gettin' doors shut in your face is like the kid in the film, who wouldn't take No for an answer. Only, anyone who'd stopped to think, would realise she wouldn't dare shoot. If a tale told out of school could bust-up her plans, a bleeding corpse—and no disrespect to the ladies intended—would wrap the whole thing up in a shroud and well she knew it. But guns have a way of looking dangerous, specially in the hand of a dame who's desperate . . . Come, what was it she said that drove you over the border? Maybe she suggested you had an interest yourself . . ."

Beverley Carr sprang to her feet. "No, no—you can't . . ." Avery's hand pulled her back.

"Keep out of this, Beverley," he said.

She looked at him in amazement. Like Henry in his youth, she had thought, but without Henry's compassion, Henry's tolerance. And now even his youth seemed obliterated, the skin stretched tightly over the fine-shaped skull.

"He's torturing her," she muttered, trying to fight free.

"He's trying to save Henry," replied Avery, not relaxing his grasp.

"Well, Miss B.?" insisted Crook, inexorable as the Recording Angel.

Addie had sunk her face in her gloved hands; her hat slipped a little crooked over one coiled grey plait.

" When the police come asking questions, just you remember that Mrs. Foster produced the gun before you went for her. Anyone can act in self-defence. That's the advice I'd give any client—any outsider for that matter—in a jam like this. Well, there it is. By the time the police break in the paper's gone and whatever the paper hid has gone, too, and who's going to suspect quiet, respectable Miss Bainbridge of murder? You tell me."

" Only you," whispered Addie. " Only you."

She stared round the circle. Sumner and Garland looked like men turned into stone. Mrs. Shrubsole said, " I can't give evidence that I saw her going down the lane that night. It was too dark. I thought it was a man. . . ."

Mrs. Fanshawe was staring. " It's all wrong," she exploded.

" If you say so," Crook broke in, " but—save that for the police. Maybe they have different ideas about murder from you."

Addie's big hands scrabbled at the catch of her bag; she fished desperately for something. Crook made a crablike dive, and wrested the little tube from her fingers. Addie gave a sound like a screech and blacked out. In a second Avery was on his feet.

" O.K.," he said sharply as Sumner followed his example. " I can cope."

He picked up the distraught woman and dumped her on the couch. Across the room he caught Beverley's eye and nodded. Beverley rose obediently and came over.

" She may want someone to hold her hand when she comes round," explained Avery. He looked at Crook, who sat hunched like a great red bear beside the table. Avery leaned his tall shoulders against the chimney-breast.

" Satisfied? " he inquired. " I can't say I like your methods, Crook, but . . ."

" You'll have to put up with 'em," retorted Crook, grimly. " You dragged me into this, and I do things my own way."

Mrs. Fanshawe thrust herself forward. " I don't understand," she said. " How did Miss Bainbridge know she couldn't come in by the front door? "

" Because the front door was shut," explained Crook, elaborately. " Henry Greatorex had shut it."

" I know that. But—how did she? Because she never came back to the front door. Lu—that's my sister—and me were watching, and after Mr. Greatorex went in at half-past eight no one else came down the street till Mr. Garland here arrived at nine o'clock, and couldn't get any reply. We were watching, and we couldn't have missed her. So—Mr. Crook—*how did she know?* "

It was Avery who answered. " She didn't," he said simply. " She didn't know because she hadn't any reason for wanting to come back to the house. She hadn't left a paper there, or anything else, because she hadn't been inside the house that night. Whoever Sumner heard talking to Mrs. Foster it wasn't Miss Bainbridge. He said he heard the unknown call her Stella—he heard it twice—well, Miss Bainbridge would never have called her by her first name. Most likely she didn't even know what it was. And if she had, she wouldn't have used it. So—where are you now? "

There was a moment of aghast silence. Then Mrs. Fanshawe said, " But if it wasn't her, then—who? "

" What I like about having a brother lawyer on the set is that he can dot the i's and cross the t's that have somehow got overlooked," commented Crook, blandly. " I might have guessed you'd rumble me. No, you're right, it couldn't have been her, could it, because, come to think of it, the bus from Martindale only runs once an hour—ain't that so?—and the last bus leaves at nine thirty-five. And we know Henry Greatorex was on that bus, though he picked it up a bit farther on. I know he was wearing his thinking-cap and it was a wet night and so on and so forth, but I don't believe him and Miss

Bainbridge could travel on the same bus—a single-decker, remember—and neither of them notice the other. No, I think Miss B., came back on the eight thirty-five, like she said, and of course that puts her out of court for the star role.

The figure on the settee stirred, opened her eyes and looked about her in a perplexed manner. Beverley put out a kind hand.

" It's all right, Miss Bainbridge. You had a little faint, but . . ."

" Maybe this is what you want," suggested Crook, opening his big fingers and releasing the little phial he had snatched a few minutes earlier. " Frozen eau-de-cologne," he said. " Is that what the ladies use nowadays instead of smelling-salts? "

" Eau-de-cologne? " repeated Mrs. Fanshawe. " But I thought . . ."

" You thought it was the dose of poison they used to wear in rings in the time of the Borgias. But you were wrong. Why should a lady like Miss B. want to carry poison around? "

" You said—you said she had killed Mrs. Foster."

" A chap in my position," said Crook, " has to examine all the possibilities. Well, now she's out of the running and Sumner's out and, of course, my client's out, and you have an alibi—your sister and your husband— and Mrs. Shrubsole has Mr. Shrubsole and kitty, and Avery here was out with the dog—so who does that leave us with? Only Mr. Garland, and you know what Holmes used to say. Eliminate the impossibles and whatever's left is the answer. Well, Garland, how about it? "

" You're out of your mind," exclaimed Garland, staring. " Five minutes ago you were building up a case against Miss Bainbridge."

" And now Mrs. Fanshawe and Avery between them have demolished that, so I've got to look elsewhere."

" It's no use looking in my direction. I didn't get inside the house. Mrs. Fanshawe can testify to that."

" She can testify that you didn't get in by the front door, not the second time."

" The *second* time? "

" That's what I said. We know Mrs. Foster was dead when you came back from the Horn of Plenty. That was a good point of yours, honey," he added, turning to the fascinated Mrs. Fanshawe, " about X not going to the back door till he knew he couldn't get in by the front." He turned back to Garland. " It was you who left it open first time, I suppose, and how were you to guess there'd been another visitor since you made your getaway? But you were pretty desperate, weren't you, you had to get in, and again I don't think it was to fetch the newspaper, but something else you'd brought as a present for the girl-friend. Stockings, maybe, or . . . You told the police you'd brought a little something, I recollect."

" I brought her a present, yes, but I never had the chance of giving it to her, because I didn't get in."

" So you just had to carry it around with you all evening? "

" Yes. If you want to know what it was, it was a nylon blouse, rather a nice thing from Paris. I wanted to take her something special . . ." He stopped as Mrs. Fanshawe leaned forward.

" Come again, honey," offered Crook.

" He wasn't carrying anything that night," she said. " Not a paper, not a box, nothing. And don't tell me it was in your pocket," she added, fiercely, " because you couldn't get a box big enough to hold a blouse in your pocket."

" Maybe he just had it wrapped up in a bit of paper," murmured Crook. " Or maybe he's given it to another girl-friend." He laughed, a lopsided chuckle that wasn't funny at all. " That was what you went back to fetch, wasn't it? That was why you had to get into the house, even if it meant smashing your way through the back door."

Garland thrust his hands into his trouser pockets. " I quite see you want to put someone in your man's place, and you don't care who it is. But you won't get me there. It's true I wasn't carrying anything that night, because I'd left the box in the car."

"You thought that one up at pretty short notice," Crook told him, sceptically. "You were expecting to meet her at the local, you said, and you thought she'd have eaten so you weren't going to suggest going out to dinner. You had it all set to see her home, so why leave the *bonne-bouche* in the car? It don't add up, Garland, really it don't." He surveyed the young man, without pity. "But it would fit in with the visitor Mrs. Shrubsole saw going down the lane. Round about nine o'clock you called at Number 17, found the door locked, walked up the street and went down the lane. Mrs. Shrubsole . . ."

Shrubsole leaned forward to say, "My wife has already explained to you that she cannot positively identify any particular person. It will be quite useless to put her in the witness-box and ask her to give evidence on which a man's life may depend."

"It's what's going to happen all the same," said Crook, grimly. "I don't say she can identify Garland here, any more than she could have identified Miss Bainbridge, but if it wasn't you," and once more he switched back to the driven victim, "what were you doing that night between six-thirty and eight? It was eight o'clock when you reached the Horn of Plenty, but you'd left your hotel before six-thirty, because there was an important message and you were gone before it arrived. You had about twenty miles to cover on a good road without much traffic. You should do it in thirty minutes, say, which 'ud get you into Martindale round about seven o'clock. Well, you didn't go straight away to the local, not either of them. There was no smell of you till eight, and even if you made a long trip of it you've still got about an hour to account for. And actually, you didn't make a long trip, because the attendant at the car park remembers you coming in at seven o'clock. He'd just come on duty . . ."

Garland bared his teeth like a backing horse. "You've over-reached yourself at last, Crook. You couldn't have talked to the attendant, *because there wasn't anyone on duty that night at seven o'clock*." He glared round him triumphantly. " You all heard him. And if necessary I can get proof it's a lie. There wasn't anyone on duty."

If Garland was like a backing horse Crook was like a ratting terrier that sees its chance and jumps in to fasten its teeth in the enemy's spine.

" How come you're so sure—*unless you were there at seven that night?* And if you were there at seven, where were you at seven-fifteen and seven-thirty and seven forty-five? I'll tell you. You were at 17 Hallett Street. You waltzed up and rang the bell and out comes your lady-love. She's expecting the boy-friend, see, and she opens the door—it wasn't on the latch then, you can bet your bottom dollar, she had a thing about open doors, my client told me so—and she begins to say, ' Come in, sweetie-pie ' and then she sees it ain't the sweetie-pie she expected. Mind you, you didn't realise that, not right away. You've sent a card, see, and you don't know it ain't arrived. That's me, you tell her, and here's a thing and a very pretty thing, and who's the owner of the pretty thing? That's the box with the blouse in it, and you drop it on a chair and the newspaper on top of it, and—was it then you noticed a drop in the atmosphere, not quite the warm welcome you anticipated? Never mind, I can answer that for myself. Naturally Mrs. F. ain't going to fall all over you when she's got a real winner coming to call. Took you a minute or two to get the hang of things, I dare say. Then it gets through to you—you ain't wanted. Didn't anyone ever teach you to take hints from a lady? If you'd made your getaway then you wouldn't be sitting here now wondering how the heck you're going to escape the rope necktie. Still, if everyone could see round the next corner no one 'ud ever get found out at all, would they? Another thing. You said you left a message at each of the locals to say, if Mrs. F. turned up, Pete was asking for her."

" Yes."

" I don't get it," confessed Crook. " You didn't go

back to either of 'em. You didn't say you were goin'
to visit her . . ."

" It was only when I found she wasn't at either that
it occurred to me that she might be waiting for me at
home."

" At nine o'clock? "

" It was possible."

" And when you arrived you found the light on—well,
you could see that, couldn't you, even if the curtains
were drawn? Mrs. Fanshawe and her sister saw it the
next day—and you knocked and you rang and nobody
came, so you went away."

" That's right. I went straight back to my hotel."

" Didn't try and get in touch with the lady next
morning? "

" I had to be off at eight o'clock."

" That was convenient for you. What did you say
to the lady the night before that made her produce the
gun? "

" I don't know anything about a gun, except what
I've read in the papers."

" Or maybe it was the other way round," continued
Crook, undeterred, " maybe it wasn't you trying to soak
her but her trying to touch you."

" Touch me? " Garland stared, genuinely amazed.
" She wouldn't have had a hope. I just about break even
on the year, that's all. Besides . . ."

" Well? "

" She had kind of a secure atmosphere round her.
I didn't think she ever lay awake at night wondering
how to settle for next quarter's rent."

" Well, of course, you know she didn't," agreed Crook,
reasonably. " You knew she had a gentleman friend that
she was expecting that night. All the same there was
some argy-bargy about money. Mr. Sumner here overheard it. Lady said she was hard up."

" She wasn't talking about money," exclaimed Garland,
contemptuously.

" Maybe she was saying she wasn't so hard up for

company that she had to hang around waiting for a drummer—all right, all right," as Garland stormed to his feet. " I only said maybe. And on my sam," he added, candidly, " if you put that look on your face I'm not surprised she drew out the little gun. Did you know it wasn't loaded? "

" To tell you the truth, I didn't stop to look. I know those little Martini numbers, and when I see one pointing straight at me—and not even the safety catch up—Oh, no . . ."

He stopped, staring about him. He had been flabbergasted enough when Stella whipped out her little gun and told him to stay speechless if he valued his life, but not so much as now when he realised that his crafty adversary had bagged his wicket at last.

CHAPTER XII

THE NEWS was splashed all over the press next morning.

FOSTER MURDER SENSATION
MAN CONFESSES:
"I KILLED MRS. FOSTER."

For good measure the more highly-coloured organs added a quiz of their own.

MRS. FOSTER'S DEATH
MURDER OR ACCIDENT?

The statement of the accused would not, of course, be released till after the trial, but Crook was permitted a private view. It was very much as he had supposed. Garland had reached 17 Hallett Street shortly after seven o'clock, taking his welcome for granted. It took him two or three minutes to understand that his card had not yet arrived and that Stella's preparations, the pretty dress, the fresh flowers, the hospitable whisky bottle, were none of them for his benefit. When he did appreciate the situation he said coolly: " Ditch this chap, whoever he is. First come, first served." " Don't talk like that," said Stella sharply. " Of course I'm not coming out to dinner with you." Still he didn't recognise his danger. " How about letting us meet and fight it out? " he proposed, with a grin. Crook, a quicker reader than the unfortunate Peter Garland, would have read between the lines before this, realised that to the woman her unexpected visitor was no more than a fill-up. Besides, she wouldn't want a scandal, anything that might get back to Henry Greatorex, and Sumner was no fonder of looking a fool than the next man. " I want you to go," said Stella, crudely for her. " Give me a drink, anyway," suggested Garland. " I can help myself." And then he'd laughed and said. " What's it all about, really? Expecting the police? " They were still arguing, but matters hadn't entered the zone of tragedy when they heard the click of the gate.

" That's my friend now," said Stella. " I told you not to stay. You must go out by the back."

Her sitting-room was divided in two by a pair of curtains; she explained quickly how to go through the kitchen into the little passage and so out by the back door that led to the lane.

Peter Garland suddenly lost his temper. " I'm damned if I do," he said. " I was good enough for you when it suited your book."

She must have guessed then that she was playing on a losing wicket. All she could hope for was to persuade Sumner that this fellow had smashed his way in, on the strength of a casual meeting at the Coach and Horses and was making himself objectionable. She began to shout.

" I suppose she wanted her friend to think she was in danger of rape or murder," said Garland to the police. " I tried to calm her down but I couldn't get a word in edgewise. Stella, I'd say and again Stella, but it was no good. The funny thing was—we both knew there was someone else in the house and we were waiting for him to open the door. And nothing happened. ' All right,' I said, ' let him come in,' and I went towards the door. In a flash she'd opened a drawer and she had the little gun in her hand. ' Leave that door alone,' she said. I couldn't believe it at first. ' Don't be a fool,' I told her. But she wouldn't stop talking. ' What makes you think I'm so hard up for company I'd want you here? ' she said. It was as though she'd gone demented. I knew what Sumner meant when he said it was like seeing a person you believed you knew turn into someone quite different. Her hand was shaking, and I thought the gun would go off, whether she meant it to or not, so I jumped in to take it away and—she fought me, but I knocked it out of her hand and then—I had hold of her, I was shaking her, and suddenly I knew she was dead. I knew it, but I didn't believe it. It didn't seem possible. I'd seen men die in the war, but this was different. After a minute I remembered the fellow in the hall. He must have heard her raging, know she was threatening me, and there was the gun to show it. I shouted out, ' Come in, don't be shy, it's all over—all over! ' And still nothing happened. I opened the door and—there was no one there. I wondered if we'd both gone mad, imagining footsteps, but I knew we hadn't. There had been someone there, someone who hadn't wanted to get mixed up in a mess and had crawled out. That shook me. Till then I hadn't meant to hide the truth. Now I saw the way it would look to the police. Even now, if there'd been a telephone on the premises I'd probably have rung through, but there wasn't, and that gave me time to think. And I began to wonder if I couldn't crawl out, too. So far as I knew no one had seen me come in, and the Invisible Man wouldn't want it known that he'd been skulking in the hall. Anyway he didn't know who I was. I didn't want to do anything but get out. There was no sense looking for my card because Mrs. Foster had told me it hadn't arrived. If I could make it seem I was expecting to meet her in the local, as I always did, I thought I had a chance of ducking from under. I hadn't said anything on the card about coming to the house. I wiped off my prints from the handle—I hadn't touched anything else— and I slid out. I didn't want to attract attention, so I pulled the door to—you had to slam it because it was swollen by the damp—and there wasn't a soul about. The windows opposite were dark. I thought luck was with me. I went along to the Horn and asked if anyone had seen her; they hadn't, of course, but I hung about for a while, and then left a message that I was going on to the Coach and Horses. Here I had a nasty shock because I met a chap who said he didn't suppose Mrs. Foster 'ud be coming along, she had a friend visiting her. He lived opposite and his wife had seen someone turn in at the gate. That put the wind up me. I tried to tell myself I hadn't left any clue, when suddenly I remembered the newspaper—they were talking about the railway accident and that put it into my mind. The paper didn't matter, because I didn't see how they could trace that to me, but I'd taken along a blouse in a cardboard box, and in the hurry and alarm I'd forgotten all about it. If that was found on the premises my number was up. It was a new line my firm was putting out. I might just as well have left my visiting card. I didn't know what to do. Then it occurred to me that perhaps this chap, whoever he was, might not notice the door wasn't quite shut, and when he didn't get any answer he might go away. In that case I could be first in the field, collect my parcel and then give the alarm. It was risky, but I was in it up to the neck anyway. If there was a policeman there already I'd bought it, but I couldn't see that I could be any worse off for walking down Hallett Street. The lights were up in the windows of the house opposite, but no one else was about, no police cars, no ambulance, nothing. I went up and walked through the gate and rang the bell for the look of the thing. Then I pushed the door and I found it was shut. That was a facer. It occurred to me that the Invisible Man might have been watching, and as soon as he saw me clear out he could have moved in. I rang, but nothing happened. I decided that my first idea had been right, that X had gone in, found the body and got away at once, not wanting to have his name connected with the affair. If that was so all I had to do was collect my evidence and follow his example. Obviously I couldn't call the police, because they'd want to know how I'd got in. I remembered what Mrs. Foster had said about a back door. I walked away a bit ostentatiously, because I knew I was being watched from the house opposite, and I thought it would help me if I had a witness to swear I hadn't got in. I went down the lane at the back—I nearly ran against someone at the corner, and I know now that must have been Mr. Greatorex, but he didn't seem to want to attract any more attention than I did. I didn't know about Mrs. Shrubsole at the window—the light wasn't strong enough to shine on to the lane—and if I had it wouldn't have made any difference. I found the back door unlocked—I didn't think anything particular about that, I didn't think of anything but getting hold of the blouse and getting away—I didn't even look at Mrs. Foster, except to note she hadn't moved, so I felt pretty certain no one had got in. I got out and back to the car park and drove off. When I got back to the hotel they told me about the telephone message that had come just after I left. I made rather a fuss saying it was too bad, there'd been a muddle and I hadn't met my friend after all, and it was a pity I hadn't stayed in a few minutes longer. There wasn't anything in the papers the next day, so it seemed improbable she had been found. The suspense was terrible. In a way it was a relief to see the news. I still didn't see why I should come under suspicion. I had no fear of the Invisible Man and I didn't believe that anyone else had got in. I never meant to do her any harm, I liked her, I just wanted a jolly evening. When it was over I couldn't believe what had happened. Even now it doesn't seem as if it could be true."

A not particularly edifying common-or-garden story, Crook found it. Garland had had bad luck, and a competent counsel should get a verdict of manslaughter for his client. Take it by and large, he reflected, Sumner came out of it as badly as anyone. No amount of influence would be powerful enough to keep his name out of the case, and no one likes the chap who slinks off and leaves another fellow to take the rap.

" May find himself in the cart yet," Crook confided to Avery Greatorex. " Suppression of evidence, see? "

" Had he any evidence? " asked Avery. His face was dead-white and he seemed thinner than ever. Crook realised what he'd look like when he was Henry Greatorex's age, the same good looks, the same charm, but with lines of responsibility carved into his features that Henry would never know.

" Evidence? " repeated Crook, astounded. " Ain't you a lawyer? His evidence would have got my client the benefit of the doubt. Mind you, he couldn't have proved that Garland put out the lady's light, but he could have shown he had the chance. No jury 'ud have dared bring in a verdict of Guilty with that story in front of them."

" That wouldn't have helped Uncle Henry much," Avery suggested, " or Beverley either. There'd always have been chaps who'd have wondered which way the truth lay."

" My job isn't to establish the truth," Crook pointed out, grimly. " It's to get an acquittal. Still, as you say, he's in the clear now."

" Tell me one thing more," said Avery. " Was Miss Bainbridge in the plot? I mean, was that faint a bit of play-acting? "

" You ain't doing yourself justice," reproved Crook. " Really, you ain't. No one who knew the lady would believe she'd let your uncle spend five minutes in prison if she could pull him out. She'd have run so fast to put her own head in the noose even I wouldn't have been able to stop her."

Avery nodded and uncurled his long length from the stool. " I'm glad about that," he said. " It confirms me in what I've suspected for a long time. I'll never be a lawyer—not single-minded enough."

Crook watched him go with an unwonted pang in the heart beating so sturdily under the brightly-coloured waistcoat. He liked his life, wouldn't have changed places with the Grand Cham of Tartary, assuming there was such a person, but now and again, to-day for example, he faced the fact that there were other ways of living and some of them might be even better than his.

But he didn't let it trouble him. Let the dead past bury its dead, and he was what circumstances and his own choice had made him, and on the whole he didn't complain. He finished his drink and settled the score for the pair of them, and went back to the Old Superb. He liked to tie up the ends neatly and he still had to face his final interview with Henry Greatorex.

Henry looked ten years older; he was smooth and cool

and politely grateful to Crook for all he'd done, but some change had taken place in him. Crook supposed, reasonably, that no man could pass through this sort of ordeal without its leaving its mark.

" All set for wedding-bells? " he inquired, cheerfully, as he rose to go.

Henry shook his head. " There's a time for everything, and if you oversleep there's no going back. Fifty-one's no age to marry a girl of four-and-twenty, and I wouldn't want Beverley's children to know their father had once been held for murder. It's the kind of record only a monster would want to hang round his son's neck. Remember that line in the New Testament about the rain falling on the just and the unjust? The innocent suffering along with the guilty? I thought I'd die for Beverley and perhaps that's still true, but I couldn't stop her being hurt almost to death. I've done her enough harm."

" Take a word of advice from a confirmed bach.? " suggested Crook. " Don't leave the lady's point of view out of the picture. Nothing makes 'em so savage, as you should know (really the fellow had no delicacy at all), as being treated like a parcel of merchandise. Consult Arthur Crook, the matrimonial agent. I know what you're thinkin'. Here's young Avery ready to hand, as like you as your own son might be, the right age, no murky past . . . You may be streets ahead of me in the law game," continued Crook blithely, not, of course, believing that for a moment, "but you don't understand women, pal. They don't switch over so conveniently. If this gal has taken a fancy to become Mrs. Henry Greatorex nothing's going to stop her—certainly not you. And my bet 'ud be that she has. As for young Avery—now, *he's* my cup of tea. He don't want a cosy home life, he'd be a bull in a china shop in that kind of set-up. Nor he won't stop on in Beckfield, and wouldn't, apart from all this. He ain't the type. Any day now he'll be out once more on the old trail, his own trail, the out trail, you mark my words."

He was talking to Henry in Henry's own flat, and as he finished speaking he got up and walked across to the window.

"Talking of angels," he said, "here she is, and if all angels looked like her there'd be more competition for the straight and narrow path."

He nearly crushed Henry's hand in his own leg-of-mutton fist and went out. Beverley was waiting by the lift as he stepped out of it.

"Little Sir Lancelot's all set to do the big martyr act," he warned her. "So if you want to change your mind, here's your chance."

Beverley put her hand on his arm and staggered him by kissing his hard red cheek.

"Knock me down with a feather," gasped Crook.

"That's for our guardian angel," said the girl, gently. "Mr. Crook, if Henry had died I should have died, too. He's my whole life and, without him, I wouldn't have anything left worth preserving."

"He's hooked," reflected Crook, philosophically, turning into the bar of the Castle, "and young Avery will get over it. He's not like his uncle at heart, he's the real martyr type, never happy unless he's being uncomfortable. Well, that bein' so, he's chosen a very good time to get born."

He moved across to the slot telephone and a moment later was blithely beseeching the last of his Rum Old Girls to come and have a quick one with him.

"Thank you, Mr. Crook," said Addie Bainbridge. "I will."

THE END

>>> If you've enjoyed this book and would like to discover more great vintage crime and thriller titles, as well as the most exciting crime and thriller authors writing today, visit: >>>

The Murder Room
Where Criminal Minds Meet

themurderroom.com